NOW I
LAY ME
DOWN
TO DIE

NOW I LAY ME DOWN TO DIE

Elizabeth Tebbetts-Taylor

COACHWHIP PUBLICATIONS

Greenville, Ohio

Now I Lay Me Down to Die, by Elizabeth Tebbetts-Taylor
© 2018 Coachwhip Publications

Published 1955
No claims made on public domain material.
Cover image: Sleeping woman © Miramiska

CoachwhipBooks.com

ISBN 1-61646-432-1
ISBN-13 978-1-61646-432-5

NOW I LAY ME DOWN TO DIE

1955 DUST JACKET

CHAPTER I

Mira Hira had a headache. She was struggling quite desperately not to admit it to herself or to anyone else at Mira Hira, Exclusive Gowns, Hollywood.

Mira, perhaps because of her highly temperamental and quixotic clientele, had a genuine horror of anything even remotely neurotic. And she knew that her sturdy, sensible Irish mother, Sharon O'Hara, would have labeled such nonsense as shilly-shallyin'.

Mira, born plain Moira O'Hara in a cheap tenement in Chicago, had come a long way, but she still held to her simple principles. Shortly, she might even be able to afford headaches—of the Floren Lawrence variety, for instance—but for the present, and until the divorce was settled, she had to make full use of her Irish wits and her Irish tenacity.

Blindly her square, well-manicured hand, ringless now, went out to a slab of white push-buttons, miraculously found the right one to summon the particular genie she desired, and punched it down carefully.

In a moment the thick blond wood door opened to admit a brown-haired young woman, smartly coiffed and dressed in black, with the thick patina of a flawless, expertly applied makeup like a cloisonné mask over her narrow classic features.

"You rang, Miss Hira?"

"Yes, Alma," replied the woman sitting at the tortuously modernistic blond desk. "Who is waiting for me?"

"Mr. Renwick is in the foyer. I told him you were very busy, with the fashion show and all—"

Mira tried to conceal the stab in her heart. Alma, with her wide, curious eyes, mustn't see that her husband's name could still affect her in any way.

"Yes," she said in a voice so cold and flat that it frightened her. "He'll have to wait. Who else, please?"

"Well, Floren Lawrence is here demanding that black evening gown you promised her for the Vardaz' premiere Saturday."

"I told her not to expect it till Thursday. This is only Tuesday."

"I know. But—well, she is odd at times."

"Odd!" said Mira, raising raven eyebrows. "How near ready is the gown?"

"She can have a fitting."

"All right—put her in number nine in the tower. That's at least isolated, and if she throws one of her fits—well, the rest of the house won't know it. Serve her tea or a cocktail and stall her awhile. Have the fitter ring me when she goes up; I'll come for moral support."

"All right," smiled Alma. She consulted a small notebook. "The only other one is a fashion reporter from the Clarion—Mabel Stimms." Alma made a face. "Wants to see you about the fashion show next Monday."

"Show her in," said Mira promptly.

In the short interim she nervously re-arranged the few items on her desk—the buff blotter, the jade cigarette box and ash tray, the phone, the leather-framed picture of her ten-year-old son, Sean, taken in his military school uniform and looking out of eyes not one bit like hers, but exactly like Ian's. She glanced out the window at the red hibiscus bush that flowered profusely there, and then the door opened.

Mable Stimms might look like a fool in her careless tweeds, flat shoes and thick-lensed glasses, but she had been and was an astute reporter who, coming lately from the East, had taken the only available perch on the complicated Clarion ladder—that of fashion reporter. She was forty-nine, with cropped grey hair, blunt nicotine-stained, type-ridden fingers and a deceptively mild voice and manner.

"Miss Hira?" she all but whispered.

Mira rose, the gracious hostess at once. "Yes. Please sit down, Miss Stimms—this one is the most comfortable. Cigarette?" She lighted the newspaper woman's and her own and took a chair opposite her guest instead of behind the desk. "It was very nice of you to call."

"Well," began Miss Stimms in a slightly more audible tone, "naturally everyone in fashion is interested in your new show. Could you give us a forerunner, or a slight preview?"

Mira smiled.

"We're not ready yet for our preview, so I can't give you much— but perhaps one or two gowns are nearing completion, if you can wait?"

"Oh, yes!" said Miss Stimms. She rose at once, for which her hostess was extremely grateful. Alma appeared in the open doorway.

"Show Miss Stimms to the foyer, Alma. I'll send for her."

Alma nodded and left. Mira lowered her head to her hands.

Alma reappeared in a few minutes, but by that time her employer was ready for her, calmly perusing a batch of mail.

"Mr. Renwick is very insistent," panted Alma. "He says—"

A cool voice from behind finished for her. "He says he must and will see you at once, darling. No excuses accepted."

Mira glanced up, her heart in her mouth, and saw Ian leaning there in the doorway. That was the trouble with him: he never stood on his own two feet.

Mira narrowed her dark eyes as Alma discreetly left the room and closed the door.

Ian was completely unaffected by this treatment. He grinned at her impishly, pulled the two leather armchairs closer together, and draped his long slender length between them not without grace.

"My sweet, this is all ridiculous," he told her.

"You know how I feel, Ian."

"No. I only know how Jamieson says you feel."

"I feel exactly that way."

"Do you, darling? Do you really!"

"Yes, I do." Mira's voice was getting a trifle shrill.

Renwick laughed.

"We're beginning to sound like a page of dialogue from one of the more wretched modern novels, I fear." He unwrapped his long length and came across the room to her desk.

Mira forced herself not to stiffen at his approach, not even when he laid a hand lightly on her shoulder. "Look here, old girl, we belong together, you know. I may have my faults, but you have a few barbs yourself, darling—thorns on the rose, eh?"

"Ian, I don't wish to discuss this with you any further. Conrad Jamieson is handling the matter for me."

Renwick removed his hand from her shoulder, and a note of harshness crept into his voice. "I would handle the matter myself first, if I were you, Mira."

She turned in spite of herself; his long, thin face with the pale brows and high-bridged nose was uncharacteristically tense and purposeful.

"What do you mean?"

"I mean that a divorce, at this time, is going to cost you a great deal more than you anticipate. Look!" Suddenly his face slackened into its habitual indolent mask; his voice resumed its lazy, insolent drawl. "We're not enemies, you and I. We've been married eleven years—and there's Sean."

Mira felt her face stiffen. "Sean," she said, "means nothing to you. He never has."

"That's where you're wrong, my dear." The grey eyes so like Sean's own mocked her words. "After all, Sean is my son, as well as yours. A father may neglect his duties, let us say, even his personal responsibilities, but that doesn't make him any less conscious of being a father."

"If you're worried about Sean at this late date I can't see that it's very touching. I will be given full custody, you know that. Of course," she added roughly, "you can see him when you want to."

Ian bowed solemnly. "You were always a generous girl, Mira darling."

"Then, if you're satisfied, I can't really see what all this is about. I have people waiting, Ian; I must ask you to go." She began hurriedly to gather up papers, her pen, a green lizard notebook that went everywhere with her. The "log book," Alma jokingly called it.

A discreet knock, followed by Alma's curious cloisonné-surfaced face, interrupted them.

"Sorry," said Alma, "but the fitter is just about ready for Floren Lawrence. Fifteen minutes or so, she said."

"Thank you, Alma. Who's going up?"

"Maggie."

"Fine. Tell her not to worry; I'll come and help her beard the lioness in her den. Is she biting nails?"

Alma grinned. "Oh, no! Gay as a lark. She's been holding court. Male and female!"

"Male?"

"Yes. Edgar Vorman is with her—and a Mr. Rossi, who brought her. In the chips, I would say. His car is something out of this world—one of those foreign jobs, all swirls and curves and two blocks long. There's a crowd out front looking at it. Think I'll join them!"

"Rossi," said Ian Renwick. "Is that Duke Rossi?"

"I don't know, Mr. Renwick."

"Well, I haven't seen Floren in ages; maybe I'll pay my respects to the lady before you strip her, Mira."

Mira told Alma in her cool, businesslike voice, "Send Billy up to them with refreshments, Alma, please."

Alma nodded and closed the door with discreet reluctance.

"Well," said Ian, "I suppose all of this has been in vain." There was a petulant, harassed note in his voice.

"I'm afraid so. Please run along now, Ian."

He put an arm about her shoulders, and she went as taut as a violin string. "No farewell kiss—for old times' sake, Mira?"

"No! Please—"

He released her slowly and stood twirling his hat in his hands. "Very well. I know I've behaved like a cad in lots of ways. I suppose the trouble is that we couldn't or wouldn't understand each other. Understanding is a priceless possession." He glanced up at her and smiled. And for a moment she saw the man she had loved and married so long ago in Chicago, when she had been a little designer apprentice in a very fashionable dress shop. Ian had accompanied a wealthy dowager, a friend of his mother, to their fashion show. Ian had just arrived—or been sent out from England. The family gave him a meager allowance. For the rest he got by on his charm and connections. His connections also had put Mira in business for herself and made the present Mira Hira possible. She felt suddenly deflated and miserable. If only he'd been a different sort of person—or she had.

"Goodbye, Mira." He was holding out his hand, a hand that had never done a piece of work in its life, a smooth white hand, but muscular. She put her own square-tipped one into it. He pressed it, then raised it to his lips. "I haven't given up trying to circumvent this thing, darling," he warned her, one fair eyebrow raised, "nor shall I."

"It's no use, Ian."

He smiled, turned to the door and opened it. She could see Alma's desk in the little reception room beyond. It was vacant. Alma's lucite desk clock with the modern dots for numerals said 4:15.

"By the way," called Ian, "do you mind if I pay the boy a visit at school?"

"No," said Mira. "Of course not."

He grinned and was gone, through Alma's room and out into the hall. Mira noted that he didn't turn left toward the big front reception room, but went right toward the stairs and elevator. Probably going to visit Billy in the bar, she thought vaguely, or up to see Floren.

Thoughts of Floren changed her at once into the competent executive of Mira Hira, Gowns. Using the house phone, she called the workroom.

Jessica Lowenstein, her chief designer and most valued employee, answered, "Yes?"

"Jessica? Mira speaking. Has Maggie gone to the tower yet?"

"No." There was a curious note of reluctance in Jessica's voice.

"Isn't the gown ready to fit? I know Floren is days early for us. I can't see why she came when we both told her not to come till Thursday."

"She can have a preliminary fitting," answered Jessica vaguely as if her mind were on another matter entirely. Then she added, "As a matter of fact, Maggie did go up a few minutes ago but she was sent away."

"Sent away?"

"Yes, I guess Floren's having too much fun drinking your cocktails and entertaining the men in her boudoir-away-from-home."

"Did Floren send Maggie out?"

"She never got in. Some man answered the door. She could hear a lot of laughing and talking going on, and then Floren shouted for her to go downstairs and wait till she called for her."

"Who is up there?"

"There was a crowd at one time, according to Bonnie Bartlett. She met Floren and company in the foyer and went up for a second. We'd just finished with Bonnie, but I guess the fancy car and Floren's exotic company were too much for her. One of them, she said, looked like a Hindu prince."

"Nonsense! Alma says Mr. Vorman and a Mr. Rossi were with her. Vorman looks like a squirrel, and whoever Mr. Rossi is I don't think he's a prince in disguise."

"Bartlett says two other men carried up some suitcases and then left."

"Suitcases!"

"Yep."

"Well, I'll talk to Billy; he'll know if he took up drinks."

"I think Billy told Maggie they made him leave them outside."

"What's going on up there?"

"You know Floren. Might as well let her have her fling. Oh, one other thing Bonnie Bartlett said something odd just before she left. She told Kathy Johnston that Floren said she had brought something for you and had something to tell you that would make a new woman out of you, and then she laughed like an idiot."

Mira said, "I'm going to phone the tower now and end this nonsense!" She hung up, noting that her hand shook.

The tower at Mira Hira's was really an afterthought, due to the brilliant ingenuity of its architect, John Willoughby. "Miss Hira," he'd suggested, "the roof's cone-shaped, but there's room to add a small tower. It will give the building added height and distinction, and provide you with an extra workroom or office." Mira had agreed, thinking first to use it as her own office. But the tower was too far away from the working units of her business and proved too bothersome to reach for both employees and clients. Alma had suggested turning it into a super fitting room for their more difficult to please clients. It had proved an excellent idea. Many customers would not come for a fitting unless they could use the tower room.

It rose above the other buildings on this section of the Sunset Strip and gave an uninterrupted view of the Hollywood-Beverly Hills panorama.

Jessica Lowenstein had used a deft artist's hand in decorating it. It was a circular room, nearly all glass, with a high-domed ceiling; she had concentrated on the magnificent view and the fact that this was a showcase for milady's gowns.

Floren Lawrence, sitting with her legs tucked under her in the center of a long blue sofa, a man on either side of her, was admiring the tableau in one of the far mirrors, quite conscious that she still, at thirty-six, looked twenty at a distance, that she was really just coming into her own as far as brains and charm and talent were concerned, and that she was a little tight.

Her manager, Edgar Vorman, straightened his small back and delicately touched the knife-crease in his gray trousers with a manicured fingernail. Other than the gray trousers, which he secretly disliked but had been cajoled into getting by his conservative business partner, Ned Haley, he presented as flamboyant a picture as a circus poster. His fifty-odd years may have had something to do with it. Old habits die hard, and Edgar had been in Hollywood at the time of its raucous birth. He clung tenaciously to the loud checkered coat, black and white sports shoes, dark glasses and beret. He even used a long cigarette holder. He had managed Floren ever since she came to Hollywood, a teen-aged beauty contest winner, just another pretty, vapid, movie-struck kid of little or no ability. Edgar alone had seen the possibilities in her and carefully nurtured them. His flower had blossomed and paid him off handsomely. It would, he thought, pay him off even more.

He turned his narrow-jawed, squirrel-like face with the puffed cheeks and shrewd, blinking dark eyes behind tinted spectacles, and ran a small, busy hand over his grey hair as he spoke to Floren.

"Darling, I do wish you'd let me handle this new deal with Mantley my way—without interference. After all, sweetheart, I know the industry like my mother, and if you would only—"

Floren frowned slightly. "I'm not going to bother with Mantley or any other contract, Eddie."

"What!" squealed her manager, jerking forward in his seat. "Darling, you're drunk. You must lie down; I'll get you a blanket and a pillow." He rose quickly.

"No."

Floren Lawrence, they said, had a beautiful voice for such a loud one. Edgar Vorman had worked long and hard to turn her fishwife's Chicagoese into clear, brittle tones. Her diction was perfect but she had never grasped modulation.

"Darling sweetheart, listen to me—"

"No, I said. Eddie, I don't have to worry about my career, as you call it, any more. I'm not going to toady to producers and directors and backers in the future."

"Eh? Now I know you're drunk, angel, or out of your mind or both!" He raised his shoulders under their width of false padding, and flung out his hands in a hopeless gesture toward the other man present, who had remained quietly twirling his glass through all this. "I don't get it," said Vorman plaintively. "Do you?"

The other man, tall and dark, glanced up briefly and then down at his glass again without smiling. "She knows her own business," he said finally in a quiet, even voice.

Edgar Vorman glanced at him suspiciously. He was reflecting that he knew very little about Duke Rossi. He didn't move in the intimate circles of the industry. Floren had met him somewhere on one of her personal appearance jaunts about eight months ago. He'd have to check.

"Look," he said, using his most dogmatic, managerial voice, "Floren, honey, how you handle Mantley will make or break you, and handling him is going to be a tricky business. Besides that, just in case you're forgetting, angel, you have other commitments. Metro and Warner's both have a picture coming; one in England, remember."

"I have my plans," said Floren with a sweeping, queenly gesture. "I don't want to discuss it now. I'm really getting rather tired, Eddie. And I have a fitting. I'm afraid you fellows will have to—"

Someone knocked at the door.

"I told them we didn't want to be disturbed," said Floren.

"I'll go," said Rossi, rising, but Vorman was before him. He opened the door a crack and then fell back reluctantly. The man leaning in the threshold smiled at them and motioned a white-coated Chinese boy bearing a tray inside ahead of him.

"Ian!" cried Floren Lawrence in her flamboyant, carrying voice. Her violet eyes opened very wide and the dark lashes rose like a fan nearly to her curved red brows. Both the lashes and the deep red brows were her own.

"Hullo, Floren. Edgar. Put the tray down there, Billy, and thanks."

The Chinese boy nodded and went out, leaving silver cups and a gleaming, crested cocktail shaker behind on one of the glass coffee tables.

Ian Renwick came over and kissed Floren's long fingers in a solemn and judicious manner. "You look like Aurora on a mountain top, darling."

He turned halfway toward Rossi, still holding Floren's hand with the flashing emerald bracelets like green fire touching his fingers, and said: "I don't believe I've met your other guest, darling."

"This," said Floren swiftly, "is Duke Rossi. Duke, Ian Renwick, Mira Hira's husband."

"Yes," said Ian, bowing, "they have never failed to add that. A title should never be forgotten, do you think, Mr. Rossi?"

Duke Rossi said nothing, but his dark eyes met the Englishman's in a level stare. Floren was thinking he certainly wasn't much help when it came to a difficult conversational moment. But he had so many other qualities that did count.

"Well," said Ian, "I see you've already been celebrating whatever it is you're celebrating in my wife's charming little ivory tower, but you won't object if I bring you a farewell toast of my own? Something Billy and I concocted to my own recipe. I call it 'Andele' in honor of our southern California clime. Appropriate, don't you know, for a farewell."

"What's all this about farewells?" grumbled Vorman, savagely fitting a cigarette into his ivory holder.

Ian walked over to the tray and began to twirl the shaker gently, his back to them. "Didn't you know, old boy, Mira and I are, to put it bluntly, in the quaint jargon of the columnists, 'an item.' We have come to the sweet parting of the ways."

"No!" said Vorman.

"Oh, yes, I assure you."

"When," asked Floren suddenly, touching her brightly carmined lips with her tongue, "did you decide all this?"

"Just now. Today. In fact, my pet, I have just now come from the ordeal a defeated and despondent man." He poured a yellowish liquid into the shallow silver cups and brought two over in his hands. "This is yours, Floren, my lovely. And this is yours, Mr. Rossi, since you are the stranger in our midst. Vorman, yours is comin' up." Ian returned for the remaining cups.

Florence put hers down and said suddenly, "I don't believe a word of it!"

Ian turned, a comical twist to his lips. "Darling! Have I ever told you a lie?"

"Yes, you—" Floren stopped herself in time and added lamely, "I just don't believe it."

Ian crossed the room slowly, gave a cup to Vorman and raised his own. "'Andele'! To the end. People drink to the beginning of love; why not to the end? Ah, well, our secret has been well guarded—"

Floren glanced up swiftly. "Darling, I still can't believe it," she said. "I am so dreadfully sorry!"

"Thank you, sweet," said Ian. "Aren't you going to drink your Andele?"

"Later, darling, after you've gone—all of you. I'm so tired—stills all morning, and interviews this afternoon. I'm dead. I think I'll curl up on the couch and sleep for an hour or so. Now run along like lambs, please?" She kissed her fingers to them.

Rossi said gruffly, "Do you want me to wait outside?"

"No, darling! After I wake up I've got to have that tiresome fitting. I could have killed them when I got word and had to come today on top of everything else! But that's life, I guess."

"I'll come back later then," said Rossi quietly. "You can ring me."

"Yes, of course, darling, I'll do that." Floren rose and followed them to the door. "I'll lock it," she said, "so they won't pester me!" She smiled at them, her famous wide, friendly smile with something of the gamine in it.

"Don't forget to drink your Andele," said Ian.

"I'll wait for your call," Rossi reminded her, putting on his hat.

"Tomorrow we'll talk," said Vorman peevishly, his little eyes glinting behind dark lenses.

They heard her laughter as she shut the door on them, and the click of a lock, and each carried a picture of her in his mind as they rode down in the small private elevator to the lobby. A picture of a tall, long-legged, red-haired woman dressed in violet, with gay laughter on her brilliantly painted lips.

The men parted in the main reception lounge, a big oval room, white and chartreuse, very modern and chic. Ian nodded to Kathy Johnston, the ravishing natural blonde who graced the white, oval-shaped counter near the door. The round onyx clock behind her shining head said five o'clock.

Mira was finishing her third cigarette and glancing at some sketches she'd made the night before when the phone rang.

It was Kathy Johnston at the reception desk. "Miss Hira, I just wanted to tell you they've all left the tower—the men, I mean. So maybe you can go up now."

"Thank you, Kathy," said Mira.

She was going to phone Jessica and tell her to send Maggie along, but decided it might be better if she spoke to Floren first. Floren was such an unknown quantity where temperament was concerned.

Mira rang the tower. It was some time before she got an answer, and then Floren's loud, distinct voice came irritably over the wire. Mira was sitting at Alma's desk in her own little reception room. Alma was out, it seemed, and Mira had decided it might be best to use her phone where she could keep an eye on the hall door—just in case Floren had some unpleasant sputtering to do.

"Hello, Floren, this is Mira. I just wondered if you were ready for that fitting yet?"

"Oh, for Pete's sake!" cried Floren. "I was just lying down. I'm completely pooped, darling; simply a ghastly day! I feel absolutely numb! I've simply got to have forty winks, Mira. I'm going to lie down here in this blessedly quiet room and open the windows wide, and sleep. Can you, like an angel, fit me later?"

"Well," said Mira, "I can wait, but I don't know about keeping the whole staff on."

"Oh, I'll only sleep a couple of hours, I promise, sweet. Besides, all you need is that fitter woman and Jessica and yourself, isn't it?"

This was true. The main staff could leave.

"All right," said Mira heavily, "but I warn you—if you're not awake by seven I'm going to wake you myself, pet!"

"Do!" There was a pause, and then Floren added, "As a matter of fact, I want a little private talk with you. I have some news for you, darling. And something important to show you. I hope it won't be a shock." She laughed suddenly, then went on, "But it's to be a surprise and I won't tell you over the phone! I have to see your face. Who knows, I might want to use the reaction in a character sometime?" She yawned elaborately.

"Don't oversleep," warned Mira again. "You'll find a robe and pillow in the hall closet if you want them. Or Billy can bring up some from the office."

"No," said Floren quickly. "'Ay vant to be alone.' Really, I am going to lock the door and go to sleep this minute. I've never felt so tired in my life." The instrument went dead in Mira's hand. She placed it thoughtfully in the cradle and stared unseeingly at a bunch of scabiosa in a vase on the end of Alma's desk. Then she rose and went back to her own office and closed the door.

She phoned the workroom again and told Jessica what had happened.

"The devil!" said Jessica. "I had a dinner date."

"I'm sorry," said Mira. "I wouldn't ask you to stay, only—"

"Oh, never mind; Saul won't. I'll phone him to pick me up later. We'll still have time for a late show."

"Thanks, Jessica. How about Maggie?"

"She'll stay."

"Good. Is the place empty yet?"

"Just about. Mrs. Yates-Wolfton is upstairs getting dressed. Nora just finished with her, but you know the Yates has to lace up her corsets. She doesn't think we know she wears 'em."

Both women laughed.

"Well, when she's gone tell Kathy and the rest they may leave. You and Maggie go out to dinner now."

"What about you?"

"I'll wait till I go home."

"Can't we bring you something?"

"No, thanks. I've a whopper of a headache. Nerves, I guess."

"Try a B.C." Jessica rang off, and Mira folded her arms on her desk and put her head down on them like a tired child. But there was no escape. Alma walked in a moment later.

"I heard all about it," she said, "and it's ghastly! That wretched woman."

"I don't mind so much. I'm almost too tired to budge, anyway."

"Want me to stay?"

"No, dear. You run along."

"Why don't you phone Francine to come for you later? Leave your car here tonight?"

"I may," smiled Mira. "Thanks for the suggestion."

"Oh, I forgot," yelped Alma. "That newspaperwoman—Stimms!"

"Don't tell me she's still waiting, poor thing?"

"I'm afraid so. In the lobby. Shall I—"

"Just send her in," soothed Mira; "then you may go. Oh, you might tell Billy to send us some tea before he goes."

"Yes, of course." Alma disappeared, and Mira went to her tidy but microscopic washroom, redid her face, combed her hair methodically and put it up again, and took a B. C. powder from the cupboard.

"I'm dreadfully sorry about the mix-up and delay," Mira was saying contritely to her guest. "You were so kind to wait."

"Not at all," murmured Mabel Stimms.

Mira, pouring tea from a silver pot and offering cookies, ad-libbed cheerfully, "I'm afraid I've another apology to make, Miss Stimms. Our designer, Miss Lowenstein, tells me we haven't a garment ready to show you yet. However, I have some of the final sketches here and I can show those to you."

"That will be fine, Miss Hira."

Mira brought a thick folio from the green filing cabinet in her office and started to explain the drawings to Miss Stimms. She soon found that they anticipated one another's thoughts to a startling degree.

"You've never been a fashion reporter before, Miss Stimms, and yet you know at a glance what is good basic and what is merely flash in the pan," she marveled.

Mabel Stimms flushed slightly at the honest admiration in Mira's voice. "I've been on papers with some of the best fashion writers. I don't know beans about which woman should wear what, but I know good design and cut when I see it." She ended up rather lamely, "This job is rather a stopgap for me. As soon as possible I'm going back to straight news; it's more my kettle of fish."

"If you'll come to the fashion show," Mira was saying, "you'll see the real models. They do make up a bit different, I must admit."

"Oh, I'll be there," laughed Mabel Stimms. "And thanks for the talk and the tea."

As Mira closed the door on her she caught a glimpse of a man's coated figure with upturned collar outside, near the entrance. Probably one of the girl's men friends, she decided, and went back to her office. Her wrist watch told her it was after six. She picked up the outside phone and called home.

Francine's comfortable, motherly voice answered her.

"Fran, dear, I'm afraid I'll be a little late, so don't wait dinner. I'll grab something when I get in."

"Nonsense! I'll wait," came Francine's warm, comforting voice. "I've a good beef roast, and it'll keep. And the rest I can do when you get here. What's the trouble, dear?"

"Floren Lawrence," said Mira wryly. "There was some mix-up over her fitting. We thought we'd told her to come in Thursday and I'm sure we did, but she insists it was today, and you know Floren."

"She's a rattle-brained, spoiled fool," said Francine tartly. "When will you be through?"

"I don't know, dear. You see, La Floren decided to sleep it off for a couple of hours in the tower, so—"

"Of all the nerve!" sputtered Francine. "I'd go right up there now and fit her in spite of herself, if it was me!"

Mira laughed. "I can't do that, darling. We have to humor her. I won't be too late, because I warned Floren I'd wake her by seven, come what may!"

"Good! Oh, Sean called up from school this afternoon."

"Is anything wrong?" asked Mira swiftly, clutching the phone.

"Heavens, no! He just wanted to ask if he could spend the week-end at Lake Tahoe with some boy named, let me see, Freddie Benson."

"Oh," said Mira.

"I didn't want him to bother you at work, dear, so I told him I thought it would be all right. I said if it wasn't you'd phone him tonight."

"It's all right," laughed Mira. "I know the Benson boy. His people have a weekend place at Tahoe."

"Well, that's about all the news," Francine chattered on. "I told the butcher what I thought of that last steak we got, and he said he'd make it good. But I mustn't keep you. Go and wake that wretched female and then come home. I'll have a hot bath, a Tom Collins and dinner ready."

"I was going to ask you to come for me, Fran, if you can. I'm dead beat; the thought of that traffic is more than I can bear."

"Of course I'll come!"

"I'll ring you when I'm finished."

"Oh, no. You don't need to do that. You're going to wake her at seven, so I'll start around seven-thirty. It won't matter if I'm a bit early? I want to stop at the library a minute anyway, and they close at nine. And I'll put through a call to Sean and tell him it's all right about Tahoe. So I can do it all nicely."

"All right, dear. And thanks."

"Phoo! I'll be in the parking lot in my usual place."

Mira hung up the phone and glanced at her watch. It was 6:21. Outside, someone walked briskly along the hall. Probably Jessica returning from dinner, thought Mira as she lay down on the couch and closed her eyes.

CHAPTER II

Mira awoke with a start. Sitting up, she rubbed the back of her neck. She shouldn't have fallen asleep. But the rest had done her good. After all, she thought, if Floren could take a nap undisturbed, why couldn't she? Glancing at her watch, she was appalled to note that it was eight o'clock.

Odd that Jessica hadn't called her. Mira went swiftly to the house phone and called the workroom.

"Yes?"

"Jessica, I fell asleep! Why on earth didn't you wake me?"

"I looked in at quarter to seven and you were dead to the world. I thought you needed the rest, and La Floren hasn't called down yet, so—"

Mira laughed ruefully. "I'm going to call her pronto! You and Maggie come along up as soon as you're ready."

"Okay."

Mira lighted a cigarette while she waited for Floren to answer the phone. The bell tinkled on and on. She's probably in one of her stupors, thought Mira. I may as well go up.

On the way out of the office she suddenly remembered that Floren had said she was locking the door. The pass-key was on her key-ring. She fished it out of her alligator bag in the washroom and went out to the elevator.

The little hall upstairs was dark. Mira switched on the lights and rapped sharply on the door of the tower.

"Floren? Floren! Wake up. It's Mira. Floren!"

Her tattoo produced no reaction. You couldn't look through the keyhole. It was a Schlage doorknob lock. Sighing with vexation, she fitted the pass-key in the door and swung it back. All the windows were open, and the room was now cold and drafty.

"Floren!" Mira called as she closed and locked windows. She could see the actress' outline as she lay sprawled on one of the blue couches. It was maddening that she could sleep like that. Mira flicked on a lamp. Then she saw the silver cocktail shaker and cups. They belonged to Ian. As a matter of fact, she'd given the set to him one Christmas after they were first married; she'd ordered it at Tiffany's and had a struggle paying for it. Ian now kept it downstairs in Billy's refreshment bar for special occasions. Obviously it had been quite a party.

Still absently looking at the tray and its contents, she went to the figure on the couch and shook it gently.

"Floren, wake up, sleeping beauty. We can't stay here all night."

Suddenly she was aware of the complete stillness of the flesh her fingers touched. Not a sound came from the blanket-draped figure on the couch. Not a murmur. Not even a sign of breathing.

Mira looked at her fully for the first time, seeing the face with a startling and rigid clarity. The thick-lashed eyes were closed now in peaceful slumber, the whole face relaxed and wiped of expression like an empty slate. The mouth had a slack, foolish look, falling away from the teeth. Mira began to tremble. Her knees felt as if they must give way. And there was a whirring sound in her head. It grew louder and louder. With a tremendous effort she held onto her reason and classified the sound as the elevator. Jessica and Maggie! She must stop them. She must be *sure.* . . .

Frantically, feverishly as in a nightmare, she felt Floren's wrist, her temple, tried to listen to her heart. Pawing through Floren's elaborate cordé bag on a side table, she found a mirror and held it to the actress' lips. Nothing It remained clear, unclouded.

She walked unsteadily to the door, pushing back her hair, just as Jessica and Maggie Tally stepped out of the elevator into the narrow hall.

"Lord, it's cold up here," shivered Jessica. She was a tall, supple girl of twenty-eight, with short dark hair and intelligent black eyes with a slightly Oriental slant. She wore a tremendously chic black and white ensemble.

Maggie Tally, by contrast, was a drab, dumpy spinster of fifty-three, with frizzled grey hair and weak blue eyes protected by cloudy pince-nez on a black cord. Her black dress was covered by a sateen apron with a red pincushion, tape measure, and scissors dangling on a string from a pocket.

"I should say it is," murmured Maggie. Her nearsighted eyes peered up and down the hall. She stooped and picked up a bit of fluff on the hall rug and put it methodically into her apron pocket. "That janitor doesn't half clean up here, Miss Hira. You ought to speak to him."

Maggie, like so many people who are careless about their personal appearance, had a mania for neatness and order around her. Her apartment was a spotless citadel.

Jessica moved forward, the long lengths of black chiffon and net trailing over her arms, and took hold of Mira's cold hands.

"What is it? What's happened?"

Mira raised her eyes to meet the designer's.

"Floren. She's dead."

Jessica stiffened. "You're sure?"

"Yes."

"Dead!" cried Maggie breathlessly. "But how could she—"

Jessica was thrusting the unfinished gown into Maggie's ample arms; turning, she disappeared into the tower room. Mira and Maggie followed slowly like sleepwalkers.

Jessica's slim back was bending over Floren as they entered. When she straightened up the others looked at her expectantly.

"She's dead all right."

"I spoke to her on the phone at six," said Mira.

"What was it—heart?" Maggie asked in an awed whisper.

Jessica frowned. "Can't tell." In a practical voice she said, "We'd better call the police, Mira."

Mira nodded.

Jessica walked briskly to the little desk near one of the windows and took up the phone. She turned then, saying, "Someone's just driving in the parking lot."

"Probably Fran," murmured Mira. "She said she'd come for me. Maggie, would you go down and tell her what's happened?"

Maggie paused to fling the dress she still held onto a chair, and then literally ran from the room. They heard the purr of the elevator and then Jessica's voice, clear and precise, went into the phone: "This is Mira Hira's gown shop, on the Sunset Strip. We've had a sudden death here. No, no doubt at all. Yes. Yes, I understand. This is Miss Lowenstein, Miss Hira's designer. Thank you."

She hung up and came across the room to Mira. She put an arm about the latter's shoulders. "It's just one of those things, Mira."

"You don't think she did it on purpose, Jessica?"

"Not considering the high spirits she was in today."

"But this is so very sudden!" Mira felt the hot tears gather in her eyes and begin slipping down her cheeks.

A warm voice at the door said: "Don't cry, darling. She wasn't worth it."

Turning, Mira saw Fran's welcome, plump figure through a blur of tears and stumbled forward into her alms.

"There," soothed Francine. "There, there, pet! I know it's horrible for you. It's a shame she had to die here. Heart, I suppose, or a stroke."

"We don't know," said Jessica. "Maggie, if you'll stay here, I'll go down and let the police in." A faint wail could be heard in the distance. Jessica went out and closed the door.

"I wonder how long she's been dead," said Maggie. "Was she cold?"

Mira flinched. "I don't know."

"Of course not; it was too much of a shock," said Francine firmly. "The police will tell us anyway." She laughed. "This is my night for police."

"What?"

"That's why I was a bit late, dear. The phone rang just as I was going to the library. It was only a wrong number, of course; don't see why we get so many. Then I was in a hurry to get into the library, and I bumped a fellow's car while parking. It was as much his fault as mine! The fool man was pulling out from the curb as fast as you please, and without a hand signal or anything. I was heading into the place he'd just left when another car—really, these Los Angeles drivers!—came along, and the fellow who had started out had to back up, and of course, I drove right into him."

"Any damage?"

"Well, I dented his fenders and rear lights a bit," admitted Francine unhappily. Everyone knew that Francine was a wretched driver.

Mira patted her plump hands.

"The worst of it," blurted Francine, "is that a policeman happened to be parked across the street and saw the whole thing, and he claimed I was to blame! Can you imagine?"

The door opened and Jessica entered, followed by several men in plain clothes.

"The police," said Jessica. "This is Miss Hira, her housekeeper, Miss Webb, and our fitter, Miss Tally."

The chunky red-faced man who led the others came across to Mira. "Captain Reame of the sheriff's office. Mind telling me what happened?"

Mira gave him as concise an account as she could.

Reame watched her face solemnly, listening in respectful silence, hands in his pockets.

The other men went straight to the couch and bent over Floren's body. In a moment Reame joined them and they consulted in low tones.

Reame returned presently.

"Is there some other place we can go and have a talk?"

Mira nodded. "My offices are downstairs."

They filed out, leaving the other men to their odd ritual.

Reame politely held doors for the women and allowed them to precede him. Mira felt relieved that he was not one of those rude, bullying officers she had heard about.

Reame put his hat on her desk, and with a nod sat down behind it and took out his notebook. He was slightly bald. He plucked a pen from a breast pocket and unscrewed the cap.

"This is your shop, Miss Hira?"

"Yes."

"Been in business long?"

"Ever since I was twenty-three." She smiled faintly. "I started in Chicago as a designer. But we moved to this location six years ago, and I opened my own shop."

Reame nodded and put a cigar between his thin, brick-red lips. Freckles stood out like sawdust on his broad hands and wrists as he wrote. Apparently he didn't intend to light the cigar. It rolled idly between his lips.

"Known Miss Lawrence long?"

"Almost ever since I opened here."

"Old friends?"

"We were acquaintances. She was a valuable client. I am in business, Mr. Reame. We were not close personal friends."

"Of course." He turned to face Jessica, Maggie and Fran. "The rest of you acquainted with her?"

"I knew her in the shop. That is, she came as a customer, and naturally, working here, I came to know her in a purely business sense." Jessica's long artist's hands were slack on the chair arms. But there was wariness in her dark eyes.

Maggie Tally said hurriedly, "I fitted her—oh, hundreds of times. A lovely figure she had! And she always liked my work. Of course she was hard to please—wanted everything just so, you know. But she remembered to thank you when you were through." Maggie dabbed at her eyes.

Reame took down her full name and address and those of the other women and told Jessica and Maggie they could go home.

Mira, feeling as if she had been put through a wringer, clung tightly to Fran's soft, plump hands. Fran's pleasant voice was saying, "I'm afraid I don't know her at all, poor thing. I don't come to the shop. Of course, I knew Miss Lawrence on the screen; I love the movies. Sean and I go nearly every Sunday. She was a wonderful actress, if you like the sort of sophisticated things she plays in.

"Was it heart, do you think?"

Reame did not reply, but made a notation in his book. Just then the phone rang at his elbow. He picked it up, and Mira said: "No, the other one. That's the outside line."

Reame took up the other instrument and held it to his ear. "Yes? Uh-huh. All right. I'll be up pretty soon." He replaced the phone, methodically closed his notebook and restored it and his pen to the breast pocket of his coat.

"This is going to be hard on you, Miss Hira," he said. "They've found out what Miss Lawrence died of."

"What was it?"

Mira could feel Fran's hands pressing hers. "She died of morphine poisoning."

The words rose in Mira's brain, gigantic blood-red letters etched there for all time. And then when she thought she couldn't bear it another moment, everything blacked out completely.

CHAPTER III

Her first conscious thought was that there was something cool and moist on her forehead and covering her aching eyeballs. She could hear voices, too. At a distance somewhere. There seemed to be a great deal of activity in the hall, unfamiliar footsteps pounding up and down, doors opening and closing loudly. Then it all came back with a sickening rush.

Mira sat up and thrust the damp towel from her face. She was alone in her office. A coat had been thrown over her. A glass of water stood on the table beside her. She reached out with trembling fingers to grasp it, and drank slowly. The muscles of her throat began to relax a bit and she stood up.

Behind her the door to Alma's office opened and closed, and Francine came in bearing a pair of glasses on a tray.

"Don't try to get up yet, dear," she said at once. "Here, I found the brandy in Billy's bar. After all, if you have to pay for a liquor license in this place, you may as well get some good out of it yourself."

Mira drank the brandy like a dutiful child, curled up on the sofa. Fran sipped at hers. For the first time Mira began to feel warmth in her hands and feet. It was like coming alive again.

"How long was I out?"

"Not long, darling. Please don't look so frightened, Mira. There's nothing to be afraid of!"

"But he said—"

"Just that they'd found out how she died."

"Nothing more?"

Fran shook her head. "They don't give out much."

31

"Do they think it was an accident?"

"I've no idea. Furthermore, we aren't going to discuss it. Inspector what's-his-name said I could take you home and he'll talk to you tomorrow, which is sensible, I think. Now come on and get into your coat, dear." Mira obeyed, putting her arms in the grey wool coat that Fran held for her. She watched Fran struggle into her own dark tweed coat. Fran, she decided, looked like a round, mature cherub, prematurely grey-haired. She was all circles and curves—not an angle in sight. Soft round pink cheeks, candid grey eyes, short curly grey hair making her round face even rounder. She ought to have married, Mira thought, and had five kids. I've selfishly kept her tied to me and my troubles for years. It's not fair. Just because we were once roommates is no reason for her to feel duty-bound toward me.

The hall was crowded with men. Several of them swooped down on Mira, and flash bulbs popped while she tried to shield her eyes. Fran jabbed at them with her oversized handbag that she always carried, and crowded Mira out the back entrance, bolting the door after them.

Mira's house in Bel Air was built along the side of one of the higher hills. Through wrought-iron gates her private road wound in circles for a half-mile through the five-acre tract. She and Ian had designed and built the house after their third year in California, when success seemed no longer a gamble but a certainty. Mira loved the house and intended to let other things go in the divorce settlement in order to keep it for Sean and Fran and herself.

Though the house was a large one of fifteen rooms, it had been so designed that only a minimum staff was required to run it. There was a Japanese gardener who came up daily on his neighborhood rounds, and a cleaning woman who came in once a week. The only servant who lived in was Emerald Patrick, the colored cook-maid. Actually Fran, who adored it, did most of the cooking.

"I hope Emerald left the garage open," said Mira wearily.

"Darling, did you forget? This is her night off."

"Oh, of course. Well, I'll get out and open it." She raised the heavy overhead door and watched Fran edge her blue Chrysler coupé inexpertly into the garage, scraping the edge of the door on her way. She followed her in and shut the door, bolting it in place.

They climbed the stairs to the back hall and Fran clicked on lights as she walked through the house. Through the spotless white all-electric kitchen, the orange and brown breakfast room that overlooked the terrace, on into the main hall, past the library and den, into the long living room with its sweeping wall of glass windows overlooking the lights below.

Mira sank into a chair while Fran lighted soft, rose-colored lamps and touched the thermostat on the wall to start the gas furnace. "Keep your coat on a minute until it warms up," she said. She went into the den and busied herself, clinking bottles and glasses. Presently she returned to place a tall amber-colored glass at Mira's elbow.

"Drink this," she said. "I'm going upstairs to run your bath; then I'm going to bring you a tray. Something light, I think. The roast will keep till tomorrow." She bustled out and disappeared up the gracefully curving staircase with its shallow marble steps and thick white frieze carpeting, looking both worried and determined.

Mira had finished her drink by the time Fran's voice floated down from upstairs.

"I'm all ready for you, dear. Coming up?"

"Yes," shouted Mira. "Right away."

She noted that it was after ten as she went out to leave her glass on the kitchen sink.

Ian Renwick, in a wine silk dressing gown, paced the long living room of his apartment on the tenth floor of the Saracen Arms located on upper Sunset, and glowered down on the indolent young man who sprawled, whiskey glass in hand, on his best sofa. The hour was close to one A.M.

"You are," said Renwick savagely, "either the least informed newshound alive, or else the most ungrateful! I've given you, in the past years, valuable lead after lead. And what do I get in return?"

"Well," blinked David Pierce, "I came straight to you with what I had. I delivered the scoop before it broke—officially."

Renwick snorted. "You brought me a garbled account, which I trust for the sake of your readers' palates you will refrain from forcing down their throats—but what about details?"

Pierce sipped his whiskey sedulously. "There are no details, my friend. Reame himself isn't sure. One of his boys admits that so far they've found no container, unless she kept it in her bra or girdle, or tossed it away before she used the stuff. And there was no note either at her home or at Mira's. They know you and Duke Rossi were with her before six."

"I've heard rumors—but exactly who the devil is Rossi?"

Pierce raised thin eyebrows. "You don't know?"

"No."

"He's one of the big racket boys on the Coast. All on the up and up, so he claims. Gambling in Las Vegas. But the cops keep an eye on him."

"Where did Floren meet him?"

"Jealous? She was your girl friend once, wasn't she?"

"Shut up!" breathed Renwick, gathering his fists in his pockets.

"Well," said Pierce, watching him carefully over his glass, "Duke paid off a gambling debt for her in Las Vegas. Besides, he's a good-looking bohunk."

"You swear you've told me everything that happened there to-night—everything Reame said, even off the record?" Renwick's voice was a bit taut and strained.

"Sure."

"If I thought you'd come to me just to add a fillip to your story, Pierce—"

Pierce rose, standing taller and bigger than Renwick. "I'm leveling with you, Ian. Reame didn't say it, but I know it must be going to be homicide. No note—in good spirits—dates for later. What do you think?"

"Darned if I know. She was all right when we left her. Said she was sleepy and tired. Rossi promised to call for her."

"Then she might have taken it or been given it earlier?"

"I don't know," frowned Renwick, reaching for a cigarette. He flicked a gold lighter.

"Reame will be rounding you all up in the morning," warned Pierce in a not unfriendly voice.

CHAPTER IV

William Reame ate an early breakfast at a drive-in on Wilshire Boulevard on Wednesday morning. He had already collected the first morning editions before sitting down at the empty counter where he ordered orange juice, buckwheat cakes, bacon and coffee. He placed a well chewed but unlighted cigar butt in the nearby ashtray before opening the *Clarion* to the first news report. He was disgruntled to find a picture of himself putting his foot clumsily into a police car.

"Quite a good likeness, don't you think?" asked a cool voice over his shoulder.

Reame turned and then grunted, "Oh, it's you."

The tall young man behind him twirled a stool around and perched on it. "What's left of me," sighed David Pierce.

"I didn't think newshounds breakfasted this early."

"We," said Pierce, "work for a living."

"Can it," growled Reame. "You boys've been riding the sheriff's office long enough. Pick on someone else for a change!"

"Okay, Reame. Nothing personal. Maybe the breaks have been against you, but you're in good company."

Reame savagely buttered wheat cakes, while Pierce ordered coffee and doughnuts from a sleepy-eyed counter boy.

"It's going to homicide, isn't it?"

"You know I've got nothing to say!" Reame's brick-colored face grew even redder. "Go peddle your paper."

"Going to call 'em all in this morning?"

"Pierce—"

"Now wait. Reame, I've always played it straight with you, haven't I? Even done you a favor or two—"

Reame made a strangling sound in his throat. "What do you want, Pierce?"

"A simple statement."

"I gave one out last night."

"And this is today. Old news is as dead as Floren Lawrence—you know that. But I'm fair-minded—I believe in something for something. I hear more gossip than you do, in your narrow, sheltered life. So, for what it's worth, Floren was reportedly Duke Rossi's new gal friend. There's a rumor Ian Renwick—Mr. Mira Hira—was her bojangles before that, and the said Renwick was facing divorce on the strength of it. And it also comes over the grapevine at Hollywood and Gower that Floren was sacking her Svengali, Edgar Vorman.

"There's a lot of motive mixed up in that scuttlebutt. At best, Floren Lawrence was not famous for her discretion. Hollywood may adore publicity, but it shuns scandal as the plague. It's ruined more careers than age, talkies, or two-million-dollar adaptations of best seller novels."

Reame stirred his coffee and stared moodily into the minor whirlpool it made in his cup. He was thinking that maybe Pierce could be useful in a couple of ways.

"What do you expect in exchange for this world-shaking, original theory?"

Pierce grinned back at him. "The real statement—when you're ready. Exclusive."

"You know I can't promise that!"

"Ah, but yet another plum remains in my pie, friend. Wouldn't you like to know which one of your little suspects is either so scared or so curious that they intend to beat you to the punch? Joseph Pratt Miles got in on the plane from Frisco half an hour ago."

For an instant the two men stared over their coffee cups like fencers over crossed swords; then Reame reached for a fresh cigar and put his cup neatly in its saucer. He bit the end off of the cigar, spat it on the rubber-tiled floor between them, and said, "How'll I reach you?"

The reporter took a card from his pocket, scribbled on it briefly and tucked it into Reame's pocket. "This will reach me any time. It's private—and I'll be waiting. So long, pal, and good hunting."

Joseph Pratt Miles sat as stolidly as a wooden effigy of one of his ancestors, quietly erect in a leather armchair that faced his employer in the latter's comfortable living room. He had been listening to a surprisingly clear and concise outline of the events leading up to the death of Floren Lawrence.

"I want to know exactly what happened up in that dress emporium," said the other man grimly. "And I want to know faster than the cops can get the answers. Floren was no suicide. I know that!"

"Perhaps the police agree."

"It might be easier for 'em to palm it off as suicide—there've been too many unsolved deaths in L.A. lately. I want the truth, see?" said his employer darkly. "I hear you're good at this sort of thing Funny, I suppose—me hiring a dick. But I've always found there's a time and place for everything." He lowered his voice. "Floren was—well, a pal of mine, see?"

Joseph nodded. For a full-blooded Nez-Percé Indian, his skin was only slightly darker than that of the man sitting across from him. Both were in their early forties, tall, lithe, dark-haired and black-eyed. But where his employer possessed the soft, expressive eyes of the Latin, Joseph's were the long, unwinking ones of the Indian, flat and hard as obsidian. The bones of his face, too, were more prominent. Yet many people who were unaware of his origin took him for Spanish or Mexican.

He wore a well-cut gray lounge suit, a white shirt, a discreet tie in blues and grays. His only jewelry consisted of a slightly ornate wrist watch and band in platinum, the gift of a grateful superior during his stint for G-2 during the war.

His voice had a low, quiet cadence, like stones rippled by slow-moving water. "I'll do what I can, Mr. Rossi. It will be necessary for me to turn any final pertinent facts over to the local authorities, however."

Rossi broke the ensuing silence with a sudden explosive laugh. "Okay, Miles. I don't care what you spill to the cops. But since I'm

paying you, I guess I have a right to the same information at the
same time."

"Yes," agreed the Indian.

"Then it's a deal." Rossi tossed his cigarette stub into a silver ashtray on the round glass-top coffee table between them. "Now, how
can I help?"

"I want to meet the other people who were with or near Miss Lawrence on Tuesday—if possible without them knowing my identity."

Rossi got to his feet to pace the long, comfortably furnished modern room that formed part of the penthouse atop one of the newer
Beverly Hills apartment buildings. "That's easy. You can pass as one
of my boys. Howard Mantley, the big-wig producer, is giving a shin-
dig at his place tonight. Everybody who can will get in somehow, by
invitation or crashing. It'll be quite a brawl. Believe it or not, I've got
a nice engraved genuine invitation. Floren wanted me to take her.

"Got any tails or a Tux with yuh? If not, you can borrow some of
mine. You're about my build." Rossi beamed down on his guest like a
delighted schoolboy. "Now let's eat breakfast."

Mira found the staff behaving quite as usual that morning, if not
the customers. Kathryn Johnston nodded to her and smiled briefly in
her usual manner. Billy Wong, on his way to the hall, grinned; and
Alma Roberts, already at her desk and on the phone, winked one eye
slowly and suggestively and saluted with her fingertips. Everything
at Mira Hira's was as usual—on the surface. And then as she entered
her private office she was brought up with a start. A strange dark
man was sitting in one of her leather guest chairs. He rose slowly,
stiffly, and spoke without smiling.

"I'm Duke Rossi. I want to talk to you about Floren."

So this was the Hindu prince the girls had spoken of? Mira was
disappointed. He was just a plain, dark Latin, Spanish or Italian, with
rather large, expressive dark eyes. He wore an expensive and flam-
boyantly cut navy blue chalk-stripe suit. There was a white carnation
in his buttonhole, a diamond on his little finger.

Mira nodded, went to her desk and put down her things. Seated,
she regarded him coolly and said: "Just how can I help you, Mr.
Rossi?"

"You were her friend," he blurted out. "I want to know what enemies she had."

"None, as far as I know. But then I really know very little about her private affairs. And you are quite mistaken about our relationship, Mr. Rossi. Floren was not a friend of mine; she was a customer. That is all."

"Not friends, huh?"

Mira shrugged. "As a person I liked her well enough—"

"She was a square dealer!" said Rossi abruptly.

"Was she?"

"You got something against her?"

Mira lifted an eyebrow. "No. Not now. But as I suppose you'll learn sooner or later, at one time she rather attracted my husband. It made me hate her once. But all that's long past. I was divorcing my husband."

"I know," said the gambler. His dark eyes held hers for a moment. "He told it upstairs—last night."

"Oh."

"You're still divorcing him?"

"Yes."

He seemed relieved. In a quieter voice he said: "Someone got her, Mrs. Renwick—or should I say Miss Hira?"

"Miss Hira will do here."

"Okay. I'm going to find out who done it—did it." He looked abashed. "And nothing's going to stop me!"

"I wish you would find out," replied Mira firmly.

"Do you know anything you could tell me that would help?"

Mira shook her head. "I only wish I did." She told him briefly what had occurred the night before.

He nodded, and a moment later he rose from his chair. He was very tall, much taller than Ian. His eyes, black and hot, blazed down on her. "I'm going to get whoever did this," he told her fiercely.

"I hope someone does," said Mira simply.

Duke Rossi strode to the door in what seemed to Mira like two tremendous strides, suddenly wheeled and said abruptly, "You're okay, sweetie-pie."

Before Mira could open her mouth he was gone.

The phone rang, and Mira, taking up the outside instrument, heard Sean's shrill, boyish, "Mom, is that you?"

"Yes, darling! How are you?"

"Fine! But how are you? Gee," he lowered his tone to a hoarse whisper, "I cut class to come 'n phone you after I saw the papers this morning. Gee!"

Mira spoke gaily but firmly. "Nothing to worry about, darling. Just an unfortunate accident. Everything here is under control."

"Oh." Sean sounded disappointed. "You don't want me to come and be with you?"

"No, thank you, dear, there's no need. And you're going to Tahoe for the weekend, aren't you?"

"Yes, but—"

"Go and have fun. I'll send you a money order—a small one—and you can do as you please with it."

"Golly, Mom, that's swell!"

"Be good, darling, and please be careful on the lake. And phone me when you get back."

"Sure, Mom."

She made a kissing sound over the phone and let him go, just before Alma entered carrying a huge florist's box.

"You must have a new admirer," she told her employer.

Mira jumped up and slipped off the thick blue ribbons. "Who on earth—" She found the card. It said simply, "For a sweetie-pie."

"My gosh," said Alma, glancing over her shoulder, "who in the world sent that?"

"Can't imagine," said Mira, keeping a straight face. Mr. Rossi must have stopped at the florist's across the street, she thought. "Ian, I suppose," she said carelessly.

"Does he write like *that?*"

"At times—you never can tell with Ian."

Alma's cloisonné face looked disapproving. She went to get a vase, and in the end had to get two of them to hold the array of red and white roses.

Mira buried her face in them. "Aren't they gorgeous? I adore roses! Take some of them into your office, Alma."

"Not on your life," said Alma, gathering up box and tissues. "He might come in and see them and scalp me!"

Mira laughed.

Alma straightened up and said soberly, "It's dreadful about last night. I wish now you'd let me stay. None of the customers except Mrs. Yates-Woliton have shown up for their appointments. She's upstairs now. But you needn't worry about the staff; they're all right!"

Mira asked, "Have you seen my log-book?"

"Why, wasn't it on your desk last night when I left?"

"I suppose so. I was pretty rattle-brained last night. I must have put it somewhere. It had all the appointments in it. Have you got today's all down?"

"Everything, unless you made a private or personal one and didn't tell me."

"Heavens no! Just give me your list, Alma, and we'll make out."

"Certainly." Alma went out, carrying the box and flower papers, just as Mira's outside phone rang.

"Yes?"

"Edgar Vorman here, Mira."

"Yes, Edgar?"

"I'm phoning from your house. Thought I'd catch you here, but your maid says you walked boldly into the lion's mouth. Bravo! But not me, darling. Can't stand the wretched pace any more, though reporters are quite civilized these days.

"I've got to see you alone, Mira."

"Edgar, I'm so busy today."

"Are you going to Howard Mantley's party tonight?"

"I suppose so."

"Listen! I don't want us to be seen talking together, but it's vital that I do see you. Do you recall his little Japanese tea house on the cliff? Good. Well, meet me there somehow at eleven sharp. I'll still be sober by that time, and it's important! Will you do it, like an angel?"

There seemed more than the usual urgency in Vorman's chattering voice.

"All right," Mira agreed reluctantly.

She rose and went to tell Billy Wong to take Francine's car back to her, and then she climbed the stairs to the second floor to the dressing rooms where Mrs. Yates-Wolfton was being fitted.

She could hear her one doughty customer's voice the moment she stepped out of the elevator.

"Hello," said Mira.

"Eh? Oh, it's you, m'dear." Mrs. Yates-Wolfton, a monumental Brunhilde, stood poised ridiculously on the tiny fitting dais.

The daughter of a Texas cattle baron, she had become quite pseudo-British after her marriage to an elderly and impoverished nobleman. Lord Gordon might be well into his dotage, but Margaret Yates-Wolfton was virile enough for the two of them. But for all her little vagaries, Mira had found her an astute and kindly person. She had been one of the first customers at the shop.

"This other new frock your girl's trying to sell me—it's all wrong. You can see she's got magenta. I want fuchsia—nothing but fuchsia. I have my hat all ready, a big cartwheel with velvet braid. I had it made at Mr. John's in New York, and now we can't seem to match it."

Mira joined Jessica by the window. "Well, let's see." She examined the shred of velvet resting on the bolt of moiré Jessica held out to her. "No, I can see this isn't the same shade."

"But they do blend well," murmured Jessica. "And this year exact shades are not the fashion."

"Perhaps not," bellowed Mrs. Yates-Wolfton. "but I prefer them! Blends always look off-color, hit or miss. Queen Elizabeth always matches everything exactly! I want that moiré suit to match my hat, Mira."

"Let us keep the sample and see if we can match it."

"Very well."

Mira stood watching while Maggie circled the dais on her knees, pinning up a white chiffon dinner gown.

"You won't want me for another fitting for a week?" asked Mrs. Yates-Wolfton. "Gordon plans to take the yacht out for a short cruise."

Jessica said, "A week from today will be fine for us."

"Good!"

Mrs. Yates-Wolfton was standing in the doorway puffing contentedly on her cigarette and looking like a friendly hippopotamus when they left her.

CHAPTER V

Joseph wore the borrowed tuxedo from Duke Rossi's ample wardrobe after all, and the gambler was elated at the excellent fit.

"You'd do for a double, pal," he told the Indian jovially.

They rode to Howard Mantley's villa atop the Pacific Palisades in Rossi's limousine with his correctly attired Negro chauffeur at the wheel. On the way, Rossi explained that the vehicle was also bullet-proof, sound-proof, and held a concealed dictagraph and a bar.

"All the conveniences," said the Indian mildly.

"You said it, pal."

"I would prefer that you did not use that form of salutation, Mr. Rossi."

"Huh?"

"Kindly address me as Mr. Miles."

"Look. You're an Indian, huh? Where'd you pick up all the fancy manners?"

"I was an exchange student at Oxford, and I attended Harvard."

"Oh, college guy, huh?"

"I was fortunate in having the opportunity to attend."

"Well, p—Mr. Miles, I guess I'm lucky to've hired you. Mrs. Renwick—Miss Hira—she goes for them English manners. Her husband he's English—but she's divorcin' him. He's a no good son of a—"

"What makes you say that?"

"I know!" replied Rossi darkly. He turned to stare out the thick plate glass window. "I've heard. And I've seen him."

"Just what have you heard?"

Rossi brought his gaze back from the window and fastened it instead on the dark-skinned hands in his lap. "I'm not too much better'n I should be, see? But Renwick—well, he's got two sides to his record all right, but he don't let nobody know about it. He's the smooth-type operator. He cashes in on his class, see, all the way. Dames go for that class gimmick. They like guys that can kiss their hand, and take 'em to the opera, and pick out the right kinda flowers an' perfume. Renwick's that kinda dealer. But he's smart, I'll give him that."

The limousine swerved around a stone gate and up a steep winding drive and halted behind a string of cars in a flood-lighted parking area. The house, perched a little higher, was some yards away. A rambling, three-storied pink stucco pile, with a tiled roof and only a few windows at the front, each protected by wrought iron grills and hooded by striped awnings.

As they mounted the front steps, Joseph noted that the main door was set with fine Spanish tiles about three feet wide, the whole making a mosaic picture of a fountain in a flower garden. An elderly Negro in a white coat ushered them in and wrote their names in a book on the hall table.

The hall led past closed, polished limed-oak doors to double doors that had been thrown wide open at the end. Inside was a combination ballroom and play-room. Immense, nearly as large as the Palladium, the room surprisingly and without a qualm went back to the period of the 1849 Gold Rush.

Howard Mantley had made a hobby of early Western Americana. The walls and painting had come intact from a now dusty and withered ghost town in the Mother Lode country. The bar had once graced the premises of the Bella Union on Sutter Street in San Francisco, as had the vast length of plate glass mirror behind it. There were green baize-covered gaming tables, curve-backed chairs, spittoons, an ancient piano and several large glass-fronted music boxes, and a big square dance floor was just beyond under the hanging brass chandeliers.

"Good evening, Mr. Rossi," said a voice at their elbow.

"Hi, Mantley." Rossi patted Joseph's—or rather his own sleeve. "This is a pal—a friend of mine, Joseph Miles. Thought you might like to meet him, since you go for all this Western stuff. Joe's a real honest to Pete Indian.

"Joe, meet Howard Mantley."

Joseph shook hands and found himself too absorbed in their host to feel resentment at the manner in which Rossi had introduced him.

Howard Mantley had spent the first fifty years of his life building up a fortune founded on oil, steel and railroads. Then he had retired, married a society woman, and spent the next twenty years as studiously producing and rearing a family. Then, as if this phase of his well-planned life had also come to its allotted end, he had divorced his wife—most amicably—given his four children their share of his fortune, and turned his face West to begin what he called his playtime of life. And at seventy-six, he was, if not the happiest man in California, at least the most contented.

He was a medium-sized, slender man with thin white hair, deepset mild blue eyes and a shy, self-effacing manner that was utterly charming. His voice made Joseph feel that he was honestly delighted to have him as his guest.

"A real Indian, Mr. Miles?" The blue eyes were as candidly pleased as a child's. "You will let me take him away from you for a short talk, Mr. Rossi?"

Rossi laughed. "Sure thing. See you later, Joe. I'll be at the bar."

Howard Mantley waved a slender, ringless hand at the milling throng. "You can meet them all later. I'm an exceedingly selfish host. I give my parties, you see, to please myself. For years I gave and attended parties that were more or less a necessity. Now I only give them for the personal pleasure they afford me. Come upstairs where we can talk."

Joseph followed his host not out into the main hall but into what appeared to be a cupboard. Mantley chuckled as he pressed a button in the paneling. Two sections of wall parted to show the narrow grill of a small elevator.

"I put it in to save myself climbing all those stairs. My heart is not too strong," said the millionaire. In a moment the little elevator came to a halt, and Mantley slid back the grill and pushed open a leather-padded door with a round glass window set in the top.

The door led directly into a small den or study. It was noticeably quiet up here after the din of the merrymakers below stairs.

"You are noticing the silence," laughed Mantley, pushing forward a chair. "I had the room soundproofed, the only one that is, by the way. I find that an hour of absolute silence is more restful to the nerves than several hours of disturbed solitude. We unconsciously store up the noises about us."

He opened an Italian Renaissance cabinet that had been fitted up as a cellarette and brought out glasses, a siphon and an old black whiskey bottle.

Mantley put a tray down on the leather cocktail table between them.

"Ten years ago I bought the cellar of a Scottish Earl. This," he held up the square black bottle, "is every bit as ancient as the Picts, so they solemnly assured me. However great the exaggeration is, it is a very venerable Scotch. It is supposed to be drunk straight, but if you prefer I can give you soda."

"Straight by all means," said Joseph.

"Good!" Mantley poured a tot into both glasses and handed one to his guest. "May I propose that we drink this in honor of the 'old days and old ways'?"

Joseph nodded and sipped his Scotch slowly. It was as rich and mild as butter and as potent as gunpowder. He glanced up at his host, and both men smiled appreciatively.

"Now," said Mantley, sitting down opposite him, "tell me about yourself. Believe it or not, you're the first Indian I have met. Oh, I've seen a few, but not to talk to, you understand. I am extremely interested. What is your tribe, Mr. Miles?"

"Nez Percé," replied Joseph.

"Oh! The Oregon Indians? I've read about your people. Wasn't there a famous Chief Joseph who outwitted the entire U. S. Cavalry and led them a merry chase all the way to the Canadian border before he decided to surrender for his people's own good?"

"Yes," said Joseph modestly, "he was my grandfather."

"No! But that's wonderful—simply wonderful!" The slender old man perched on the extreme edge of his chair like a fascinated schoolboy. "I greatly admired your grandfather, you know. He was an extremely astute strategist; even the military admit that."

Joseph inclined his head. He was always a little reluctant and stiff in speaking of his people, but Mantley's interest was so patently sincere that he soon found himself talking frankly and freely.

When he had finished telling Mantley of his boyhood on the reservation in Oregon, of the wealthy rancher who had sent him to Harvard, of his exchange at Oxford, the millionaire sat back and folded his hands, his blue eyes sparkling.

"Fascinating! Simply fascinating! And you took the names Pratt and Miles yourself?"

"Yes, they were the two U. S. generals Grandfather most admired. My benefactor, old Joe Cotter, also wanted me to use them."

Mantley nodded. "Do you find it difficult to return to your people now?"

"Not the younger ones. Some of the old people are a bit trying." Joseph smiled.

The old millionaire bent forward to refill their glasses. "May I ask an impertinent question?"

"What is it?"

"I would very much like to know why you are in the company of a man like Mr. Rossi?" The blue eyes were suddenly shrewd, calculating.

The Indian told him the truth as simply and quickly as he could.

"So—it's like that? The poor girl was going to do one of my pictures."

"What do you know about her, Mr. Mantley?"

"Very little, I fear." His eyes had become a gentle old man's eyes again, dreamy and remote. "She came to one of my parties—or I saw her at someone else's, I forget which. I was attracted to her, as an actress, you understand. And I told Vorman—Edgar Vorman—that when I got a suitable vehicle I would like to hire her. I know nothing about her personal life or history. But let me see if I can help. One of her great friends was the young comedienne Bonnie Bartlett, a truly clever young woman. I believe she is here tonight. At one time they shared rooms together, Floren told me. Would you care to meet her?"

"I would like to very much."

Mantley nodded, put his glass down and got to his feet. "I take it you wish to pose merely as a friend of Mr. Rossi's to these people?"

"If possible."

"Yes. I think that is best. Miss Bartlett is never at home away from a crowd. When we find her I suggest you talk to her under cover of the noise if you can manage." He smiled faintly.

"Thank you; I will."

They went down in the tiny elevator, and it was like coming from the silence of the deep onto a noisy and frolicsome shore.

Mantley smiled back brightly at the guests who tried to ensnare him in passage but kept blithely on his way until he reached one of the green baize-covered tables where a man and a woman were conversing animatedly over tall zombie glasses. The man glanced up and rose, an unusually tall, angular young man in a very inferior tuxedo, with a lazy, bored expression in his intelligent brown eyes.

"Hello—Pierce, isn't it?" asked Mantley. "Of the *Times?*"

"*Clarion*," corrected Pierce. "I crashed."

"An oversight on my part," smiled Mantley. "Please make yourself at home."

"Thanks," said David Pierce laconically, "But I've got to see a man about a dog." He walked off.

"A very abrupt young man," mused Mantley. Then, turning to the woman, he spoke gaily. "And I imagine you've seen this young lady on the screen many times. I don't need to introduce her."

Joseph gallantly followed his cue. "Bonnie Bartlett. I've enjoyed your pictures more than I can say."

"Bonnie, my dear, Mr. Joseph Pratt Miles."

Bonnie blossomed under his eyes. The clipped British accent fooled her. She thought at once of Hindu princes and obscure Mongolian potentates. She beamed up at him, her face lighting up from within as if the floodlights in a theatre had been turned on.

Mantley excused himself discreetly.

Joseph, who went to few motion pictures, had not recognized Bonnie; nevertheless she was a distinctive personality. Tall, lean rather than slender, for she had large bones and a starved, forcedly empty look, with prominent cheekbones, a wealth of shoulder length dark blonde curly hair, a creamy complexion, long straight black lashes over very large violet eyes that were both candid and shrewd. She strove to keep them innocent just as she forced her voice into precise correct speech. She was very striking in a blue sequined evening gown with real sapphires at ears, throat, wrists and fingers.

"Tell me, are you an Indian?" Bonnie asked, coyly twisting her glass with two-inch-long carmined fingernails.

Joseph smiled and nodded.

"How wonderful! I've always adored India!"

Joseph didn't correct her. Instead he ordered another zombie for her and a Scotch and soda for himself from a passing waiter.

After a short discussion of their host, the party and Bonnie's career, Joseph began casually to move in on his real subject.

"I read this morning about the death of the famous star, Floren Lawrence. Did you know her?"

Bonnie drank from her glass and said quietly: "I roomed with her once."

"I always admired her work." Joseph purposely declined to mention her personality.

"Yeah," said Bonnie. "She wasn't bad—after Ed Vorman helped her. And she had what it takes, I'll say that for her. More guts than I've got." She buried her well made up face in the zombie glass.

"What do you mean by that?" asked the Indian in as gently bantering a voice as he could manage.

"Well, I think she knew something and she tried to use it, and somebody killed her." Unaccountably, Bonnie broke into sobs. Joseph solaced her with soft words and his—or rather Rossi's—fresh white linen handkerchief. "Come outside," he suggested, sighting the terrace and garden beyond the open French windows.

She allowed him to lead her out onto the terrace and seat her in an opulent canvas swing, the awning of which was peppered with huge padded red roses.

"I feel better already."

"I'm very glad."

"You're sweet."

Joseph wanted to scotch all such ideas and said flatly, "Duke Rossi brought me."

Instead of scotching, it seemed to enhance his value.

"Really! Duke's sweet, too. So handsome—"

"Why do you say your friend knew something? This fascinates me." He sat down beside her and leaned closer.

"Does it?" asked Bonnie suspiciously. "Why?"

Joseph tried a Continental shrug which was as foreign to him as kissing a man on both cheeks would have been. "You know how it is, Miss Bartlett."

"Oh, call me Bonnie."

"Bonnie. Thank you. I'm sure you realize how interested people like myself become in all that occurs in Hollywood."

Bonnie nodded. "I guess so. It's the old ballyhoo, but it still pays off. It doesn't matter what they say about you as long as they say something."

Joseph spoke casually but swiftly. "You must have known Miss Lawrence very well if you roomed with her."

"In a way. But have you any idea how little two professional women let on to each other about their private affairs, even if they live together? Floren was a good Joe in her way—good-hearted, helpful up to a certain point. She was a lot older than I was, and when I first came here she hadn't been doing too well and was going to have to sublet her apartment in the Chelsea Arms, so I went in with her. I had a good contract, but I didn't know my way around town yet, and Floren was a big help. When she started making money again we split up. Altogether we were only together about a year."

"You liked her? As a person, I mean." Joseph gave Bonnie a cigarette from Rossi's gold case and lighted it for her.

"I've told you she was decent enough. And she was a trouper. We never clashed over a man, so we were okay. Floren could be a devil when her love life was interfered with. But I'll say this for her: she got over it as soon as she lost interest in the guy, and she never held a grudge."

"She was predatory, I take it?"

Bonnie hesitated for an instant, leaning her dark gold head back against the cushions. "Not really—not just for anything in pants. She was choosy, and moody; she never chose the same type twice. Everything had to be constantly moving and changing to please her."

Bonnie gazed out at him through half closed lashes and grinned. "She'd have gone for you, all right. You and Rossi look alike in a way. He was her latest, and I must say a change from that stiff-faced lord-and-mighty Renwick!"

"Renwick?"

"His wife is Mira Hira, the dress designer."

"Perhaps there was enmity between Mrs. Renwick and Miss Lawrence then?"

"Oh, no. They'd gotten all over that. Floren was going to Mira's for her clothes again, and she'd dropped Ian months before. When Floren was through with a man she was through. I told you Rossi was her latest flame. And it was different somehow."

"Different?" Joseph forced his voice to remain idly curious.

"Yes. She introduced me to Rossi the afternoon she died. I'd just finished a fitting and met them in the lobby at Mira's. They asked me to go upstairs to the tower for a drink. Rossi had two men along carrying suitcases."

"Suitcases?"

Bonnie giggled. "Rossi said it was pre-war bonded Scotch and he'd smuggled it in. He and Floren were celebrating something, but they wouldn't say what. The men put three quarts of Scotch outside the window somewhere, because there wasn't a cupboard, and left another one on the table for us. Then Rossi went downstairs with them."

"And you thought Miss Lawrence seemed different?"

"Yes, she did. Floren was usually rather vague about her men, but she said Duke Rossi meant a turning point in her life. She didn't go into details—she couldn't because Ed Vorman, that beastly little manager of hers, was hanging on like a leech—but I believed she meant it.

"By the way, who *is* Duke Rossi anyway?"

"I just met him myself," said Joseph truthfully.

"Oh. I thought you were both—but I suppose Howard Mantley's really the one you know?"

Joseph retained a discreet silence, allowing Bonnie to rattle on in her own fashion and make her own surmises.

"Howard's an angel, of course; everyone adores him. What I mean is, he's so terribly, terribly sweet! I never thought too much of his productions, but then he only does them for fun, and he can afford to take a loss. Floren certainly would have botched up his 'Fantastique.'"

Joseph nodded. Bonnie tossed her cigarette down the shallow steps into a fishpool beyond. "I wish," she said languidly, "that men would do the things for me that they did for Floren. But they don't. Those older gals knew how to hang onto and develop their glamour. All my generation learned was how to develop!" She laughed wryly, her vermilion lips drawn crookedly over even white teeth.

"Get me inside where there's some life, will you, honey? I'm dying."

Inside, the mingled odors of expensive perfumes, over warm bodies and liquor seemed to revive his partner while they all but suffocated Joseph. Bonnie, her violet eyes sparkling and clear, looked up at him in anticipation as the music drowned out their voices and dancers whirled recklessly up to them.

"I don't dance," said Joseph apologetically.

"Oh? But you can try. It's so easy—"

A masculine voice cut in on them, a sharp, rather rapid voice. "Darling Bonnie, do give me this one—for old times' sake? You don't mind, my friend?"

Joseph glanced down into small bright eyes and a puffed-cheeked, squirrel-like face.

"This is Ed Vorman," intoned Bonnie flatly. "Ed, a friend of Howard's—Mr. Miles."

Vorman nodded curtly and whirled Bonnie away before she had time to protest. Joseph, watching, thought that the girl's face bore a rather wary, frightened look.

CHAPTER VI

Mira decided that she was really too weary to go to the Mantley party.

Alma had laid a neat list of her appointments on the desk, and it seemed business was, if not booming, at least brisk enough to keep the staff occupied.

At four Alma came in to say wryly, "I'm sorry, but that policeman, Reame, is here again. He wants to see you."

"Please show him in, Alma."

Reame entered in his usual forthright manner, but this time he nodded to her and sat down like a man paying a strained social call. Mira came from behind her desk and sat down opposite him.

"Miss Hira, do you know anything about some bottles of imported Scotch outside the tower windows?"

"Scotch! Good heavens. No! I don't keep any liquor there. If you found such a thing someone else must have put it there—probably one of our customers."

Reame nodded. "Anyone go outside much, on that little roof part?"

"No, it's so narrow—hardly two or three feet. Wait. Billy Wong, my Chinese bar boy, or the janitor may go out sometimes to shake a rug or wash windows or fix the awnings."

"Who's the janitor? He wasn't here last night?"

"No, it was his day off. His name is Jim Jorgensen."

"Address?"

Mira rose and went to her desk. She searched a moment and finally rang for Alma.

"Alma, what is Jim Jorgensen's home address?"

Alma was gone only a moment and came back with a file card. Mira motioned for her to hand it to Reame, who copied it in his notebook. "It's a strange case," he said when Alma had gone. "We know she was murdered, and according to the M.E. report she got the dose of morphine while she was here."

He thought at first that Mira hadn't heard, she sat so stiffly silent in her chair.

"You're sure she couldn't have killed herself?" asked Mira.

"Very sure."

"But how did she take it?"

"Orally. In a drink. I understand she had several while she was here. You see why we've got to check on exactly what you were doing at every moment while she was in the place?"

Mira braced herself. She meant to tell him only what was necessary, but it would be a long and difficult interview. . . .

At seven she phoned Fran she was dining at a drive-in and would be home at 8:30 to bathe and dress for Mantley's party.

Fran said: "My dear! I do think you're wearing yourself out over this thing You're not eating, sleeping or resting properly. Please do come home as early as you can."

"I will," promised Mira. "And get out the white crepe, the new one, if it's not too much trouble."

She had lingered on at the office, however, until after 8:30, and it was 9:30 before she was bathed and after ten before she was dressed.

Mira put on perfume and was ready. She didn't have a chauffeur and she had called a taxi as usual. So, it seemed, had Francine, in her usual zeal to outdo her mistress. The two drivers arrived simultaneously and Fran admitted her mistake rather sheepishly. Mira gave the driver a consolation tip and sent him off.

And now, at Howard's, she was suddenly exhausted and the thought of further conversation, further contact with mortals was like salt on a raw wound.

"My dear!" said Howard Mantley in his soft, shy voice. He took both her hands in his thin blueveined ones and pulled her gently forward until he touched her brow with his dry lips. "You look superb! I'm glad to see you're wearing my flowers."

"I shouldn't have shown my head tonight," said Mira, twisting her bag. "But Bonnie insisted I make an appearance."

"And quite right, my dear," said Mantley. He led her away from the throng without appearing to do so, and placed her in a comfortable chair near the terrace that was partially protected by a large, glass-front music box. "We're not going to talk about what has happened, my dear Mira," said her host kindly. "This is a party and I refuse to have it spoiled."

Mira said: "I do feel like the specter at the feast anyway, Howard."

"Nonsense! I'm going to get you a champagne cocktail, and then I have a most interesting friend you must meet." He excused himself and Mira saw him speak to one of the barmen at the long, gleaming bar. A moment later a hollow-stemmed, bubbling glass was placed before her. Mira sat staring into the colorless liquid. Had Floren taken poison in such a drink?

"You know it's not supposed to be kept waiting; that's why I think of it as a very feminine liquor."

Mira glanced up into a dark, wide cheekboned but indubitably handsome face, with odd long, flat, expressionless black eyes. The man touched a chair back.

"May I, Miss Hira? Mantley asked me to come over and introduce myself; my name is Joseph Miles."

Mira smiled. "Please sit down, Mr. Miles. You must be the very interesting friend Howard mentioned."

"Let us say I am the interested rather than interesting party." She accepted a cigarette from the gold case, but her hand shook badly when she held it up for a light.

"Nerves," she said quickly. "We had a dreadful experience at my place of business last night. I'm a dress designer. A client of mine, Floren Lawrence, died under rather terrible circumstances."

"I know."

She laughed again, but there was no humor in it. "I suppose everyone in Los Angeles knows by this time. Next they'll be claiming I or one of my people are responsible."

"Are you?" The black eyes were still inscrutable, unwinking but hypnotic as a snake's.

"No," she said carefully. "I can't imagine how it happened."

"She was murdered, Miss Hira."

Mira moistened her dry lips. "Yes, the police claim that, but how—are you sure?"

"There was no container and no note. The latter is not always a criterion, but the former points absolutely to murder."

"You seem very well informed, Mr. Miles." Her blue eyes under the dark brows were frankly suspicious.

"I'm a private detective, Miss Hira. And if possible, I would like to have your help. I have been employed to find out who killed Floren Lawrence, and I mean to do so. Duke Rossi hired me."

"I see," said the woman slowly.

"And I need your help. I want you to tell me everything you can remember about yesterday from the time you got to the shop."

Mira twirled the stem of her glass.

"I suppose I'll know whoever did this dreadful thing, and it will be almost worse than Floren's death," she murmured. "I can't bear to feel that I've helped to—" She glanced up quickly and met the steady black eyes.

"Even the jungle outlaws the wanton killer, Miss Hira," he said softly.

"I know—I know! But, don't you see, if it should be a friend of mine, it will haunt me all of my days!" She covered her face with her hands.

"A guilty conscience can also haunt," said Joseph.

"Give me a little time," begged Mira.

"Certainly."

Mira looked at her bracelet watch and saw that it was ten minutes to eleven. With relief she said, "I've got to meet someone now, if you'll excuse me. Perhaps you could come to the shop tomorrow—around ten?"

Joseph nodded and pulled out her chair for her. She smiled and was gone, moving out onto the terrace and swiftly down the steps that led into the grounds, almost as if she were running away from him. Joseph, tapping a cigarette on the gold case, was thoughtful as he watched her tall, white-clad figure disappear.

CHAPTER VII

Mira walked quickly down the slanting steps between hedges and turned down the cliff path that led to the little tea house out on a natural point above the sea. She was so relieved to see the outline of the tea house that she ran the rest of the way, calling softly, "Edgar, Edgar, are you there?"

Nothing answered her; no sound came from the tea house.

Mira hesitated a moment, then thrust open the thin, carved teak-wood door. The building was square and made of sliding opaque panels set in carved teakwood, a fragile, pretty thing in the daytime. Mira recalled that there was no electricity down here. Like Howard's other collection items, this one was authentic to the last detail. She knew there were silk prints on the walls, a low altar, grass mats and a few low tables. What light there was outside filtered through the flimsy panels, but it was a murky, unsteady light at best, and becoming steadily more dim as the fog rose.

She stood just inside the door and shivered, wondering why Edgar had wanted to meet her in such secluded privacy and why in heaven's name he had selected such a spot.

Searching in the small white evening bag she carried, she found a crumpled pack of cigarettes and an extremely unreliable pearl lighter that she had long meant to discard. It had been ages since she'd used the white beaded evening bag, and the thing was probably dry. Never-theless she snapped the stem, and was mildly elated when it sprang into instant flame. She lighted her cigarette and held the lighter aloft to study the single room. It was just as she'd remembered it. She glanced at her watch and saw it was five after eleven. She hoped

Edgar hadn't forgotten about the meeting. Then her eyes fell on one of the tiny teakwood tables and she saw an old pile of cigarette ash in a cloisonné tray and a half-used book of matches. She took up the matches and the tray for her own cigarette just as the lighter flickered and went out. She went on snapping it furiously, but this time it wouldn't even spark, so she put it back in her bag and went to sit on the single wide step before the tea house. The silence and the fog seemed to vie with each other.

Finally she heard a step, unmistakably a man's step, on the path coming toward her. She rose, standing close to the house, straining her eyes. A shape loomed up through the uncertain mist.

"Edgar," she whispered hoarsely, "is that you?"

"My God, Mira! What are *you* doing here?"

That was not Vorman's chattering, staccato voice.

"Mira—"

"Ian!"

He came up the step and touched her bare arm. For some reason she drew back. She could see the white triangle of his face, the gleaming white of his shirtfront.

"What are you doing here, Mira?"

"I might ask you the same question."

He answered promptly. "I wanted a breath of unpolluted air and I wanted to be alone for a bit. Mantley's affairs are all very well if one feels festive. If not—" He let his words drift away into the fog.

"Cigarette?" he asked presently. His lighter illuminated both their faces briefly. Mira's was white and strained, Ian's calm and reflective. "What is it, old girl—what's bothering you?"

"Nothing. I just want a few minutes alone, Ian, if you don't mind."

"Did you need to come so far for them—and without a wrap? Here, take my coat."

"No!" She stepped back still further from him, inside the doorway, in fact. She felt him following her. It was very dim inside the tea house now.

"You're acting very strangely, Mira. Come back to the house."

"No! I really do want to be alone, Ian." She was suddenly frantic for some reason lest Ian and Edgar meet. "Please leave me."

He reached out and took her bare shoulders in his strong, slender hands. "Don't be a little idiot, darling."

Mira struggled and then, realizing the futile senselessness of it, relaxed. She felt herself crushed to him; when he finally released her, she was as coldly unfeeling as a stalactite. She was amazed at her reaction.

"Please go, Ian." Her voice was calm and matter of fact, something it had never quite achieved before when addressing Ian.

"Darling—"

"Ian, please."

"All right," he said in a hurt, puzzled tone. "But I swear I'll never understand you, Mira."

"You never have," she replied simply, realizing for the first time that this was true.

Suddenly Ian turned on his heel, marched down the step and on up the mist-draped path. Mira sighed in relief as she leaned against the little building and fumbled for her cigarettes.

She felt as if a great chain had dropped from her shoulders and she were free at last.

Edgar Vorman pushed Bonnie Bartlett to the other side of the love seat in Mantley's otherwise deserted drawing room and said irritably, "I'll manage you, gladly, now that poor Floren is gone, dear angel. But business is strictly business—and I'm too old a man to take what you can deal out!"

She laughed brightly. "You're frank, Edgar, darling. And rather sweet."

Edgar viewed the French clock above the Adam fireplace foggily. It was ten past eleven.

"I've got to run!" he said.

"Leaving so soon, dear?"

"I have an appointment. Be a darling and meet me at my place in half an hour—for a nightcap?"

"Can do," smiled Bonnie lazily. She was sure of her future now. Ed Vorman could do the same things for her he'd done for Floren. And he would. She watched Edgar move unsteadily across the big, priceless Aubusson carpet and out the oak door.

Mira struck one of the book matches and saw that it was 11:30. It was ridiculous to think Edgar would come now. He had probably imbibed too freely and was on his way home by now with some ambitious, fresh new starlet.

She rose, stretched and started up the cement walk, clearly outlined in the starlight now that the fog had lifted. She walked slowly because it was a stiff climb up to the house.

Halfway up the incline she stumbled over Edgar Vorman's body.

Her scream rose like an hysterical banshee's, piercing and weird in the starry silence. Then presence of mind returned and she fumbled for her bag, struck one of the book matches.

He was lying on his stomach, a pathetically small little figure lumped across the narrow cement walk, his head toward the sea. There was blood on the back of his head.

Mira knew that she was trembling like a leaf but she felt none of the giddiness she had felt before with Floren. Stooping, she touched his face. It was still warm. She hoped he was alive. She got out her compact and held it to his mouth but it remained unclouded. He was dead. She felt his body—his head. The latter was soft and pulpy in back. Her hand drew back as if it had touched a hot coal. There had been no sound, no outcry; surely she would have heard it below. And he couldn't have gotten such an injury accidentally.

Shaking violently now, she knelt again, lighted a match, and thrust her fingers into his nearest pocket. Nothing but cigarettes and matches, and a coin. Without thinking, she thrust them willy-nilly down her bosom. Voices, lights, footsteps, all were converging on her from above. She had time to straighten up and stand starkly white and wide-eyed in the first flashlight beam. The detective, Joseph Miles, was right behind the white-coated Negro butler, who carried a huge flash in one fist. Both men bent down to examine the figure on the ground.

"Miss Hira, are you all right?" Joseph took her hand and turned her away from the light.

"Yes, thank you. I found him—Edgar, I mean. I was down in the tea house—"

"Tell us about it later," he said sympathetically. "This must have been a great shock to you. Go up to the house and lie down."

"Yes, my dear child, you must come and lie down." Howard Mantley came up to them, putting an arm about Mira's trembling shoulders, and led her gently through the throng and up the path to the house.

In the main hall he touched a button and a middle-aged maid appeared.

"Vera, please take Mrs. Renwick to the gray room and see that she's made comfortable. She's had quite a shock." To Mira he said, "Go and rest, my dear. I'll find out everything and come up to you."

"Thank you," murmured Mira, and followed the stocky maid up to the second floor.

"This way, ma'am," said the maid, stepping back as she held open a door half hidden behind a tapestry that couldn't be anything but a genuine Gobelin.

The room Mira entered was a spacious, airy apartment, somewhere near the back, she judged. It was done in a soft dove-gray and white, restful and cool-looking.

Vera offered to draw a hot bath in the adjoining gray and white bathroom, but Mira refused, and the maid turned down the white and gray sprigged chintz counterpane, helped Mira off with her gown and tucked her into bed between cool sheets that smelled of lavender.

"If you need me, ma'am, just ring. The bell's on the side of the bed there. Left side."

"Thank you," murmured Mira.

The door closed softly and she was alone. After getting out of bed and locking the door, she undid her strapless brassiere and dumped the contents of Edgar's pocket, the only pocket she'd been able to reach, on the bed. She still didn't know why she had taken the things. The cigarettes were a half-used box of Egyptian Murads. Did Edgar smoke them regularly, or had he lifted them from someone? Edgar was notorious for helping himself to other people's smokes. The matchbook was a plain magenta-covered book with the initials E.V. He'd probably had them made. The coin wasn't a coin at all, but an empty keyring thing. It had a carved medallion in the center, with the usual half-circles of open metal around it. The medallion had a couple of cupids on one side and a satyr's head on the other. It looked old and worn. Mira sighed and put them in her purse.

A brisk knock at the door startled her. Her nerves would soon betray her if she didn't watch out.

"Yes?"

"Mira, darling, it's Bonnie! May I come in?"

Mira went to the door and opened it. "Come in. I'm just trying to rest."

"I don't blame you, pet." Bonnie stood outlined in the door. She was being very dramatic about it.

Mira sighed. "Come in, Bonnie. You don't have to make the grand entrance for me."

Bonnie, looking a bit sheepish, came across the room.

Mira returned to her bed, and the actress curled up on the foot, one slender, long-nailed hand curled round the carved bedpost.

"Tell me about it," she said simply. "I slipped away from the others. I had to know. Vera told me where you were. It's all ghastly."

Mira told her tale in as few words as possible, omitting only the incident with Ian and the loot she had taken from Edgar's pocket.

"I can't believe it!" wailed Bonnie. "I was with him a few minutes before. We were in the drawing room. He was going to handle me, now that Floren—oh, well. The luck of the Irish."

Mira smiled wanly as she watched Bonnie light a cigarette with unsteady fingers. Bonnie was feeling the strain, too.

Bonnie flipped back her long, dark blonde hair with a graceful movement, and looked through her lashes at Mira.

"Darling, how well did you know Floren?"

"Not as well as you did, I'm sure. She was a customer. One of my best customers. You know that."

"Yes. Only I'm thinking—and I hope you'll try to understand why I mention it—there was her little affair with Ian."

"You didn't like Floren," said Mira with sudden insight, "did you?"

Bonnie made a set business of getting lazily from the bed, walking to the dressing table and stamping out her cigarette casually in a cut-glass ashtray. She sat down on the fringed chintz-covered stool, and her eyes met Mira's warily in the glass facing the bed.

"I hated her."

"Why?"

"Because—"

The tap at the door was soft but with authority behind it. Bonnie rose to go to the door, and as she passed the bed she bent to whisper, "I'll explain tomorrow. Meet me at The Players for lunch at one o'clock?"

Mira nodded, and Bonnie went to open the door to two strange men and Joseph Miles.

Joseph entered first, smiled at the two women, and said, "May I present Lieutenant Gordon and Sergeant Jeffers of the Santa Monica police? Miss Hira and Miss Bartlett."

The two men were young and definitely bowled over by Bonnie Bartlett's proximity and pulchritude.

Gordon, the elder by a few years, was dark and beefy and wore a wrinkled grey suit. Jeffers, a slim red-haired youth, wore a uniform and carried a book and pencil in one knobby fist.

They solemnly took Mira's statement and Bonnie's statement and left, smiling politely. Joseph lingered a minute to tell the women that the Los Angeles police would no doubt enter the case and then the questioning would resume.

He came to the bed and took one of Mira's hands in his own. "You are not to worry. Several gentlemen downstairs are quite worried about you, however."

"Several?"

Joseph nodded. "Your husband, Mr. Mantley and my friend, Duke Rossi."

Mira felt herself blushing like a child. To cover her embarrassment she said rather briskly, "May we leave here now?"

"Yes, I think so. You will be available tomorrow?"

"I'm only going home," said Mira softly.

Joseph turned and offered his arm to Bonnie. "May I escort you downstairs?"

"Why, yes, I'd love it. See you tomorrow, darling." And with a backward wink Bonnie disappeared out the door on the Indian's arm, walking like a goddess. If he was a detective—well, that was glamorous, too.

CHAPTER VIII

Joseph Miles had refused Duke Rossi's invitation to stay at his swank Wilshire apartment, and taken instead a room at a nearby hotel in Beverly Hills.

Thursday, April 11th, proved to be a cold gray forbidding morning, dripping with fog and sea mist. Joseph ordered breakfast in his room, all the morning papers, and was ready to sit down at the table, bathed, shaved and fully dressed, twenty minutes later. It was exactly 7:30.

Ten minutes after that, having glanced at the papers which gave full play to the swanky setting of Mantley's superb mansion, and only scant details of the death of Vorman, Joseph rang Inspector Jim Greene of the Los Angeles Police Department at his house in Westwood. The voice that answered him was female, sleepy and indignant.

"Yes?"

"May I speak with Jim?"

"Who's calling?"

"Tell him Joe."

"What is this—Jim, Joe! Who is calling, please? I do not disturb my husband for all and sundry."

"I assure you I'm not sundry," replied Joseph mildly, "whatever else I may be. I am Joseph Pratt Miles, and I have a report for him on the Mantley case."

"Oh!" Mrs. Greene sounded chastened and impressed. "One moment, please."

Joseph could hear her talking in garbled tones, a man's grunt of reply and the sound of a receiver being passed from one person to another.

"'Lo?"

"Jim—"

"Hello, Joe!"

"I'm sorry to disturb you so early, but I think it's imperative that I talk with you this morning."

"Got something?"

"I think so."

"Not throwing it to Reame, eh?"

"There's no reason to, in this case. Besides," Joseph chuckled softly, "an Indian, like an elephant, never forgets. I still think Reame is a blunderer. He has no imagination. When can I see you alone?"

Greene seemed to hesitate and then said impulsively, "Come and have breakfast with me at the house. I'm not far from you. Westwood—711 Tanglewood Terrace, near the campus."

"I've breakfasted," said Joseph. "But I'll come for coffee, if your wife won't object."

"Gloria got over objecting the first year of our marriage," grumbled Greene. "That was twenty-five years ago."

Joseph took a taxi down Wilshire to the quiet, attractively laid out village at the foot of the U.C.L.A. campus, where they turned up one of the winding little streets pointing toward Sunset Boulevard.

Tanglewood Terrace footed the crest and made a gentle semi-circle round low, charming ranch-style houses, gay with bright flowers and verdant lawns.

Jim Greene lived in a half white-brick and half redwood siding house with tiled roof and a huge spill of purple bougainvillea over the front veranda.

As he rang the bell a honey-colored cocker spaniel dashed around the side of the house, barking shrilly and wagging his stump of a tail.

"Hello, boy," said Joseph quietly. The dog stopped barking, sniffed gingerly at shoes and pants legs, and jumped up to put both paws enthusiastically on the stranger's legs. Joseph was down on one knee rubbing the long fluffy ears when the redwood door opened.

"Gala! How on earth did you get out? Bad dog! Get in here!"

Joseph rose to greet a plump, gray-haired woman wearing a blue flowered brunch coat and cork sandals. Her face was surprisingly young and fresh-colored. "You must be Mr. Miles. I'm Gloria Greene.

Won't you come in? Jim will be right out. You must forgive me for answering you like I did—but honestly, Jim is constantly disturbed for the most trivial things! Come on, Gala!" The dog whisked past them and rushed to the rear of the house.

"I quite understand," murmured Joseph. He followed her into a small hallway and on into a long L-shaped living-dining room. It was airy, pleasant and attractively furnished in Chinese modern furniture with a great many planters on the walls, set into the floor, and even climbing cheerfully over the redwood lattice that partially divided the dining area from the living room.

"Please sit down. Do you smoke?"

"Thank you, I've just finished a cigarette. I'm sorry to disturb you at this hour."

Gloria Greene smiled. "We should be up and going anyway. Public servants aren't supposed to rest. Jim—"

At that moment Greene came into the room, buttoning up his coat. "Greetings, Joe. Come and have something with us?"

"With you, dear," corrected Gloria. "I've had my juice and coffee. I've been trying to diet," she explained to their guest, "but it's no use if I have to sit and watch Jim wolf down bacon, hot cakes and all the rest!"

"No will power," chuckled her husband.

"Huh! I'd like to see *you* on a diet for one day!"

Jim led the way down the hall to the kitchen—a long sparkling white and chrome affair with a circular padded yellow booth at the end overlooking the garden.

"Sit down," said Greene.

Gloria tried to get Joseph to eat a second breakfast and, failing this, served him tomato juice, coffee and toast, and put a heaping plate of eggs, bacon and sausage before her husband.

"More coffee on the stove," she told them, and went out, closing the door firmly on the pleasant click of crockery and the tantalizing odors of a well-cooked breakfast.

When they were alone, Green said: "What's up?"

"I was at Mantley's last night, with Duke Rossi. I had a chance to meet them all socially—and, Jim, there's something fishy about Vorman's and Miss Lawrence's deaths. I'd be willing to swear there's a strong link between them. And I'm afraid you'll have a three-ringer if you and Reame don't protect a certain person."

"Who?"

"Mira Hira."

"The dressmaker? But she's definitely one of the chief suspects. Practically made to order. She had opportunity *and* motive, from what I hear. I think Reame's headed in that direction."

"Mira Hira is an unhappy and a frightened woman. She is not a killer. The only way she might kill is in defense of her child. Even then—"

"Now you're going instructive on me!"

"She may be evading because she is afraid, or because she's protecting someone."

"Her about to be ex-husband?"

"It's possible. Or one of her friends or employees. She's a rabidly loyal woman. For that reason she's a danger to us and to herself."

"And just what do you think ought to be done about it?" Greene got up to pour more coffee from the glass coffee-bottle.

"Keep her covered and protected, without her knowledge."

Green reached for the sugar, stirred two heaping teaspoonfuls into his blue pottery cup and used what was left of the cream in a fat yellow creamer.

"We might work it out. But not because of her own danger. It's the danger to others I'm thinking of. See you later, Jim." Joseph walked to his waiting cab. It moved away.

A moment later, he said to the driver, "Thank you for waiting."

"It's okay. Don't git many calls here this early. Where to?"

"The *Clarion*—in Los Angeles. Do you know where it's located?"

"Yes, sir!"

CHAPTER IX

"Nobody but me," wailed Hector Griffith, "would still be in this sweat shop at this hour. Look at it, bare as a billiard table. Well, you want something? Speak up; what is it?"

Joseph grinned at the heavy-set, bald old man, whose eyes missed nothing and whose ears were reputed to have heard a typewriter bar miss a beat in his adjoining city room. Hector Griffith had been managing editor of the *Clarion* for forty-two years. There was a rumor his father had been alive during the '49 Gold Rush. Joseph had known Hector since they first met at the Pendleton Roundup in Oregon, when he was a boy and Hector, as a visiting big newspaper dignitary, had seen newspaper copy in the slim grandson of the great Joseph. He had done a series of articles on him. And they had kept in touch ever since.

"Well, what is it?" prompted the editor gruffly.

"I want you to give me a job."

"What!"

"Temporarily. For a week, let's say. Without pay."

"Oh. Why?" The old eyes were alert and shrewd.

"I need the prestige of your paper to help me solve a case."

"All very well. But what happens to the so-called prestige afterwards? And during the process?"

"It will be intact, I assure you. Merely send one of your ace reporters along as my running mate; then both of us will be fully protected."

"Humph! Well, let's see. Just what is it you propose to do? I won't ask what the case is—I have a good idea."

"Interview people for the Sunday supplement."

"That comes directly from the Eastern chain!"

"Then a special local page of interviews."

"My God, Joe!"

"Only for a week. Besides, it should boost your sales. In fact, I guarantee it."

"I'll bet you do! You'd scalp anybody to further your own ends—you redskin!" He laughed, pulled a phone toward him and asked, "Who do you want as a bodyguard?"

"I met one of your men last night—Pierce, I believe. At Howard Mantley's."

"Dave Pierce?" A frown creased Griffith's forehead between his shaggy brows.

"Yes. I think so."

"All right." There was caution and reluctance in his voice as Griffith began to speak into the phone. . . .

Mira awoke at 9:30 with a whopping headache. She had taken a mild sedative at 2:45 and the result wasn't unexpected. She told Fran to inform Jessica she wouldn't be in and that the latter was to make her excuses to a Mr. Joseph Miles for breaking an appointment at ten. She forced herself to eat a trifling breakfast just to please Fran. Afterwards she said:

"I'm going for a drive, dear. Don't know when I'll get back."

"Do be careful."

"I will. Oh, phone Bonnie Bartlett and tell her I can't lunch with her today. I'm just not up to it. Whatever she had to tell me can wait." She kissed Fran's fresh pink cheek, and backed her car out of the garage.

It was a gloomy morning, gray, foggy and cold. She drove down Sunset to the sea and, after pausing to watch the restless, white-foamed Pacific, turned south by instinct. Soon she was bowling along through the small towns of El Segundo, Manhattan Beach, Redondo, Palos Verdes. The latter was an exclusive spot—lovely and remote above the broad sweeping Pacific. Shaggy eucalyptus and lacy peppers lined the winding roadway. Then for miles, as the road curved and climbed toward San Pedro, it ran lonely and deserted, poised between cliff and sea, with only intermittent Japanese truck farms to break the expanse.

Mira's motor stalled halfway to San Pedro. For a time she stood in the quiet roadway, then she sat on the bumper watching, but there was no traffic. She doubted if there was much use in walking; there were no filling stations or cafés along here and probably no habitations except the Japanese farmers'. One of them might have a phone, of course. Sighing, she picked up her purse, took the keys out of the ignition and locked the car.

When she was half a mile up the road it began to rain lightly. Mira tied her silk scarf over her hair and bent her head to keep as dry as possible. In the next ten minutes the rain increased to a steady downpour. She looked around, but there was absolutely no sort of shelter. No trees; merely low scrub and cactus. No big rocks; not even a sheltering cliff shoulder. Then behind her she heard the sound of a motor tooling along at a brisk rate.

She stepped out toward the center of the road and raised her arm. She was taking no chances on whoever it was not seeing her.

The car, a dark nondescript blur moving too fast in the rain, seemed to increase speed as it neared her. Suddenly, to her amazement, she realized that it was not going to stop and that it deliberately intended to strike her. No face or figure was recognizable behind the wind-screen of sluicing water; even the little pie-shaped spaces usually left by windshield wipers were lacking. Could it be that they weren't working, that this was really an accident? But no sane person drove on even a lonely road at such speed, in a storm without visibility!

In the first startled paralysis of fear she stood like a rock, unable to move a finger. This probably saved her in the end, for the car, gauged to run her down at a certain spot, couldn't swerve fast enough to catch her as she whirled sideways in a sudden flip, and threw herself, panting and clawing with terror, into the muddy ditch beside the asphalt, her legs barely clear of the road. The car seemed to roar over her for an instant like an angry monster gnashing its teeth in the fury of having missed its kill; then it disappeared up the grade and over the hill at terrific speed.

Afterwards, Mira never knew how long she lay there, drawing breath through her teeth in gulps, her fingers clutching the gravelly, muddy ditch as if it were the outer edge of the world, all thought but a steady, numbing terror wiped out of her mind.

When she finally crawled to her knees she was as weak and languid as a new-born kitten. Road and countryside swam in her sight. She was only dimly conscious of being cold and soaking wet. Her purse lay in the ditch. She took it up mechanically in her stiffened hands and got slowly, shakily, to her feet. A glance at her watch, which was still running, told her she had lain there only a matter of minutes. Mud caked the front of her coat and skirt, and one side of her face. She stumbled forward, keeping to the extreme edge of the road. She would be safer in her car; she could at least lock herself in. Sooner or later some farmer was bound to come by and she could get help. If that same car came back . . . Her mind fought shy of the thought that someone had just deliberately tried to kill her.

She was fumbling with the lock of the car door when the sound of a motor approaching came sharply through the rain again. Her terror before was as nothing compared to what she felt now. In her haste to get safely inside the car, she dropped the keys. She fell sobbing to her knees, searching frantically in the tall, wet grass. When she knew that she could not find them in time she forced herself to sit still a moment and think. She could get to the other side of the car and probably hide herself temporarily. Scurrying like a wild creature, she crawled down between the car and the low bank. The rain and sparse grass might hide her briefly if the car drove by quickly. It was coming fast; she could hear it clearly now. Suddenly she sat up very straight. The car that had tried to run her down had disappeared over the grade ahead. This car was coming from behind her—from Palos Verdes! It meant help.

Now in an agony to get out onto the road in time to stop the oncomer, Mira stumbled and slid through the weeds, ripping her coat on the car bumper and moving blindly onto the road. She was sobbing like an animal, deep in her throat.

This car rounding the bend was coming at a fast, steady pace.

Now the car was slowing down. Twin windshield wipers were working furiously back and forth against the broad panes of glass. A door opened by the driver's seat; a man's arm appeared, a shoulder.

Mira squinted through the rain, staggered forward a step and went down in a heap in the middle of the rain-soaked highway.

David Pierce lounged against the oval reception desk at Mira Hira's while he waited for his "co-partner" to finish interviewing Miss Jessica Lowenstein. Pierce passed the time trying to crack the suave veneer of Kathy Johnston, who found nothing worthy of her attention in a mere dog-leg reporter.

"When I'm rich and famous," Pierce warned her, "you'll have to stand in line with the others, cherub."

"I doubt it," intoned Miss Johnston sweetly. "By that time I'll be in my plush-lined wheelchair."

In a small plaster-boarded cubicle off the workroom, Joseph faced Jessica Lowenstein over her neat workmanlike oak desk. There was barely room for the desk, two straight chairs and a narrow filing cabinet. There was no window, only narrow bars of white fluorescent lights on the ceiling.

So far Jessica had been polite, wary and noncommittal. Joseph was beginning to think less of his successful approach as a newspaperman when Jessica herself gave him a lead. She sat back with her spine correctly straight against her chair back and played delicately with a blue pastel crayon. Joseph thought her an extremely smart, attractive woman in her decisive black and jade green suit with a little lapel pin of diamonds and emeralds that was obviously genuine and expensive.

"If, as I understand, Mr. Miles, you want human interest material on us here, I'm afraid you've come to the wrong person. Miss Hira won't be in today, so I am in charge. I know, since we have nothing to conceal, that she would want me to play ball."

"What do you suggest then, Miss Lowenstein?"

Jessica, who was quite certain she was sending him on a profitless wild goose chase, said: "Why not interview the real characters in this case? We have a Chinese boy, Billy Wong, who served Miss Lawrence drinks that day. His angle should interest your readers. And Miss Hira's secretary, Alma Roberts. And our filler, Miss Tally, the elderly woman you saw working in the next room. And there's our shop receptionist, Kathy Johnston, young and beautiful."

Joseph smiled back at her and nodded. "Sounds like good material." He realized what she was trying to do, but he rose and held out his hand. "Thanks. I have your permission to—"

"Certainly," she smiled. I've a few calls to make upstairs, but you can have Maggie—Miss Tally for a few minutes if you care to start with her. You will use tact and discretion?"

"You have my word for it."

Jessica went out into the broad, cluttered workroom where Maggie and four other women of varying ages and sizes worked on standing forms, broad baize tables, or whirring machines, and a moment later Maggie came into the office and shut the door.

She still wore her black apron with the dangling pincushion, tape measure and scissors. She blinked short-sightedly at him as she sat down in Jessica's empty chair. Her chalk-stained fingers fumbled nervously with the blotter. But she looked amiable enough.

"Jessica—Miss Lowenstein—said you're a reporter and want to interview me." She seemed shyly pleased, like a child. "I don't quite know what to say."

"It's very kind of you, Miss Tally. Our readers just want a few words, your own impression, of what it was like the night of the trouble here. If you don't mind?"

"Oh, I don't mind. Long as Mira says it's all right—Miss Hira. She's a lamb and I wouldn't want her to get in trouble."

"Surely it couldn't cause her any trouble?"

Maggie frowned. "Well—no, I s'pose not." She bent forward suddenly, her eyes wide and serious behind her glasses. "It was just terrible, that's how it was, mister! I went up like I was supposed to and she wouldn't let me in."

"Who wouldn't?"

"Miss Lawrence, of course. Carousing, that's what she was doing, and thought nobody'd know about it if she done it here in this place! She was man-crazy, you know. I suppose she couldn't help it, poor thing. But she wanted every man she saw!" Maggie sniffed disdainfully.

"Did you know her well?" Joseph pretended to make notes in a newly acquired notebook.

Maggie watched his pencil move across the page with bird-like fascination. "Not well, maybe. But I'd fitted her for years. She wasn't easy to get on with if she wasn't in a good temper. Moody, you know. We get lots of actresses that are perfect lambs always; then there's the moody, flighty ones. You can't ever tell about them."

Joseph nodded sympathetically. "And on the night Miss Lawrence died, after she refused you admittance, what happened then?"

"I came back here and told Jessica—Miss Lowenstein—and she told me just to forget it and go back to my work here. So I did. Then she talked on the phone to Miss Hira, and she said we were to stay overtime to fit Miss Lawrence later. We went down the street to dinner, at the Copa café, and a little while after we got back Miss Hira called and said she was going upstairs and for us to follow her. When we got out of the elevator we met Miss Hira—she was white as a sheet. And she told us Miss Lawrence was dead!"

"Do you recall anything else about that particular moment, Miss Tally?"

Maggie knit her brows in obedient thought. "No. We just stopped in the hall there, and Miss Hira told us, and I guess Jessica was afraid Mira would faint, because she put Miss Lawrence's dress in my arms and took Mira by the hand or something."

"There was no other remark—nothing?"

"No, sir. Not as I recall." She laughed shyly. "I do remember telling poor Miss Hira I thought she should hire another janitor than Jorgensen. He's a lazy old man, never sweeps properly. I picked up dust on the carpet that very night—and him with a good new vacuum! Why, even in my little place—"

"And what happened after you entered the apartment?"

"Miss Hira was all upset, and Jessica took charge. Said Miss Lawrence was dead all right, and went straight to the phone to call the police. Then they sent me downstairs."

"Why?"

"To let in Francine Webb. She's Miss Hira's companion-housekeeper, and Miss Hira phoned her to come for her earlier because she hadn't been feeling well and didn't want to drive her own car home."

"Have you any idea why Miss Hira was not feeling well that day?"

"Not exactly. But I heard her husband was here—or had been. Mr. Renwick. She's divorcing him and he always upsets her."

"Thank you, Miss Tally. I may have to call on you again later, to correct my copy. Where can I reach you besides here?"

"At 746½ Star Street in Venice. I have my own little duplex my mother left me."

"Thank you," said Joseph, rising. "I'll leave you my address, too, just in case you think of any additional facts. Do you have a phone?"

"No, I don't. But the old lady in the grocery shop two doors down takes my calls. Mrs. Finch. And you can always call me here, days."

Joseph bade her goodbye and walked down the hall to the little circular bar Mira had installed for her clients. A Negro in a white mess jacket informed him Billy Wong was ill that day, and gave him a home phone number. Joseph continued on to the office marked "Miss Hira" and entered.

Alma Roberts, for her name was inscribed on a desk plate, put down the phone she had been using and eyed him narrowly. She folded her well-manicured hands languidly in her lap, and apologized for Mira's having had to break her appointment with him.

"I'm afraid I can't tell you much," she replied to his question. "I was only here a part of the evening—the early part. I offered to stay on when I learned Miss Hira and part of the staff were remaining to fit Miss Lawrence. But Miss Hira insisted that I leave, so I had no alternative."

"You went directly home?"

Alma Roberts returned his look warily. "I don't see what that has to do with your interview. I was not on the premises when Miss Lawrence died."

"It seems rather uncertain when she received the poison, however."

"Are you accusing me! Why, I was miles from here. Furthermore, at no time was I upstairs that afternoon!"

Joseph placated her as best he could, got her home address which she gave with reluctance, and made a dignified exit, joining Pierce at the reception desk in the lobby.

"If you want to ask the same questions as your friend," Miss Johnston told him coldly, "you can ask your side-kick!"

"Not very profitable?" grumbled David Pierce as they got into his battered '41 Ford.

"No."

"Where to now?"

"Either Miss Hira's housekeeper or her boy—he's at some military school."

"Yeah. Burton. Out in the valley."

"Which would you suggest?"

"The kid, I guess."

Joseph nodded.

Mira opened her eyes and said weakly, "How did you get here?"

"I have connections," said Duke Rossi. "I followed you. But not close enough. Are you all right?"

"Yes." She sat in his car, the heater on, a blanket about her shoulders. He was holding out a silver flask.

"Drink this."

She obeyed. And warmth at last began to steal through her limbs, her body, to electrify her numbed brain.

Slowly, she told him what had happened.

"We expected it," he said slowly.

"Who?"

"Joseph Miles and me," said Rossi.

"But—He—"

"I hired him to find out who killed Floren."

"Oh."

"You're cold. We've got to get you comfortable. I've got a spot near here. Belongs to one of my boys."

With an effort Mira held her chattering teeth over her tongue. They drove up over the fateful grade ahead, and then at a sudden bend in the road, Rossi turned up a narrow side trail, climbing a cliff, and they moved on for a mile or so to drop into a sudden hollow.

The house was a log cabin affair, long and half hidden beneath sheltering oak trees. A narrow stream ran by the door.

Rossi led her in, closed the thick slab door, touched a match to the huge laid fire, and lighted oil lamps. He pointed to a narrow flight of stairs and said: "Bedroom at the right—bath attached. I'll heat water and be up in a few minutes. Clothes in the closet."

Mira nodded and mounted the stairs. The small bedroom was cold and contained a narrow spool bed, a dresser, chair and night stand. The adjoining bath was a very primitive affair with old-fashioned toilet and tub. Back in her room, she was amazed to find the drawers filled with filmy lingerie. Leaving everything as it was, she sat on the bed and waited.

Rossi entered and dumped two cans of boiling water unceremoniously into the tub. She heard him turn on the cold water.

"Come on! It's all ready."

"Thank you."

"Get some dry duds on and come down to supper. I'm a swell cook! I'll pick up your clothes later to dry 'em."

Mira went into the bathroom and got gratefully into the bath. It was heavenly and restful. She soaked blissfully for half an hour. It was necessary then to don some of the closet wardrobe for dryness' sake. She selected the cleanest, plainest robe of white terry cloth. There were slippers of green leather that more or less fit.

She found Rossi, sleeves rolled up, apron across him, in the kitchen stirring up sauce. She hung her wet clothes on a chair by the roaring wood stove. "This is Italian," he said. "I hope you like it."

"It will be wonderful," she murmured.

He finished and poured the concoction into two soup plates. "Come on."

Mira ate and drank like an automaton. When at last she was warm and fed and they sat in the front room before a big crackling wood fire, she said:

"Tell me what really happened."

Duke Rossi leaned back in his deep chair, his dark eyes speculative.

"I'm ashamed to tell you—but I've been afraid for your safety. I've had a tail on you since last night. Joseph Miles agreed with me. When I heard from my tail you were headed this way, I followed. The tail got a flat in Palos Verdes. I caught up with him there, so I followed you."

Mira told him the only ideas she had on the incident.

"No one could have known I was coming on the drive, unless they were in the house. It was purely spur of the moment."

"Servants?"

"I only have Emerald and Fran!"

"Could they have talked to someone?"

"Maybe. I don't know. But who would—"

Rossi leaned forward, elbows on his knees, staring moodily into the fire. He began to speak jerkily as if words were painful to him

"Someone else could've been watching you—just like my tail." Then he said, "I know you didn't like her—Floren. Maybe a lotta people didn't. Maybe she was no good in lotta ways. But—well, she was nice to me, see? We were pals."

Mira nodded, waiting for him to go on.

"Tough breaks—well, they make ya tough, see? But they don't always turn you into a rat. I oughta know. Sure, I was a punk kid once; got hauled in. But after that I played it straight. They'll tell yuh I'm a gambler, and I am, but it's strictly legit in Nevada."

"I understand," said Mira quietly. She was strangely interested in this big, dark, oddly inarticulate man. For all his strength and power, there was something naive and childlike in his makeup. He ran a large hand through his black hair, tumbling it into disorder. Then he abruptly changed the subject. His black eyes were narrowed and calculating.

"Somebody's after you. But good." He turned to her. "Did Floren say anything to you that day?"

"Nothing out of the ordinary. It was purely business. Wait! She did make some odd remark about having something to tell me when we were alone! I didn't really pay much attention."

"Uh-huh. I think I've got an idea what it was."

"You!"

"Yeah. While we were at the Hollywood Roosevelt bar Tuesday afternoon, before I drove her to your place, Floren said something about springing a little surprise on you—about your husband. She was laughing when she said it. Then she said, 'Poor old Mira, who'd ever have thought I'd be the bearer of such tidings!'"

Mira stared into the crackling fire.

"Does it make sense?" Rossi asked. He had risen and stood with his arm resting on the stone mantel.

"No," she said. "I have no idea what she meant. She and Ian had not seen each other for some time."

"She hated his guts," said Rossi. "She told me so."

Mira said nothing. Then she asked, "Were you and Floren going to marry?"

He looked startled. "No! I told you we were pals. We understood each other! You'd be surprised, Miss Hira, how lonesome a man can get in my profession—if you get tired of the boys, see? She was good to me—kind. Not many people ever cared whether I lived or died. I don't know who my folks were; I was left on an orphanage's steps. When I got out I went to work for an Italian vegetable dealer. He wanted me to take his name, so I did. What was there to lose? He died a couple years later and left me five hundred bucks. I parlayed it into a roll at the races, started following the track. I got hauled in once on a phony play. When I got out I see there was more dough, legitimate dough, in gambling with the boys. When I got enough to buy out a deal in Reno, I came West. Been here ever since.

"Floren was the only one besides the come-on babes ever treated me like a human being instead of a deck of cards! I was goin' to back a Broadway show for her—to the limit. She was okay."

"I see. Vorman—Edgar—didn't know this?"

"No. She didn't want him to—afraid he'd cramp her style. He was a grasping little rat."

"Floren was all right when you left her Tuesday?"

"Yeah, sure. Maybe a little tight. Said she was sleepy."

"Was there any way she could have gotten the poison earlier?"

"I don't see how. They don't slip that kinda mickey in the drinks at the Hollywood Roosevelt. She couldn'ta got it at lunch with that movie reporter. And the only other drinks we had were right there at your place."

"Then you think it was—"

"Sure. Right there." Rossi looked grim-lipped and dangerous. Mira wondered if his past was as innocent or his motives as blameless as he claimed. Fear came down on her again like a smothering black net.

"You're shakin'," he said. "Wanta drink?"

"No, thank you, no." She controlled the impulse to rise and bolt from the room, and clamped her trembling knees tightly together. Her mouth felt stiff and dry. "If my clothes are dry, Mr. Rossi, I suggest we get back. My people will worry, and my car is out there."

He grinned. "All taken care of. By now your car's in Pedro, and your folks had a phone call you were delayed."

"But how—?"

"Told you I had a tail on you. Guy that got a flat in Palos Verdes. He came in here on a chance while you were takin' a bath. I told him to get your car towed and phone your place you'd been delayed, might not get in till morning."

"Till morning! Now look here, Mr. Rossi!" Mira got up stiffly and stood glaring at him.

Rossi chuckled. "Why do dames like you always jump to the wrong conclusions? And the other kind jump to the right ones—before you do anything!"

"Mr. Rossi, I intend to leave this place at once—do you hear?"

"I'm only trying," said the gambler, "to do you a few favors."

"You've done them, and I'm extremely grateful. Now if you'll—"

"Listen!" His dark face suddenly loomed closer. He was plainly angry. "What do you think I am? I go outa my way to follow you, maybe save your neck. And what thanks do I get? I'm accused of bein' a wolf on the make. Listen—aw, nuts!"

Suddenly he turned from her and marched across the room to the little kitchen. He returned a moment later with her clothes, thrust them into her arms and led her roughly to the foot of the narrow stairs.

"You got some fancy ideas about me," he said darkly. "Okay, I'll give you one to really work on." With a swift, savage movement, he arched her back and put his mouth on hers, hot, calculating and demanding. Mira, too startled to struggle, felt the fire and pain of his embrace, and then he released her and she tottered weakly. Her slap on his cheek was an ineffectual one, hampered as she was by the clothes in her arms. Tears were already spilling down her cheek when she raced up the stairs and slammed the flimsy bedroom door and bolted it. She threw herself across the bed and sobbed into the bedclothes, barely conscious that a door had slammed loudly below her on the porch.

CHAPTER X

At eleven o'clock, Joseph and Pierce pulled into a small café on LaBrea for sandwiches and coffee, and when they had finished Pierce suggested that it might save time if they interviewed Mira's housekeeper before going out to the Burton Military Academy, since Mira's place was more or less on the way.

"I don't want them to know that we're seeing the boy," said Joseph.

"Okay. You're the boss."

The Ford sputtered and labored up the long drive to Mira's home, which looked suddenly bleak and deserted in the rain that had just begun.

"Rather an isolated place," ventured the Indian as he got out of the car and stepped into the drive.

"Yeah. All these Bel Air places are, more or less. That's what they pay for." Pierce's lip curled slightly. "Isolation and privacy guaranteed. Personally I'll take a suite at the Biltmore!"

The two men walked up the steps and Joseph put his finger on the brass bell. After a prolonged wait the door was opened by a stout Negress in a green linen uniform and white apron. She looked wary and sullen.

"Yes?"

"I'm Joseph Miles, a friend of Miss Hira's—Mrs. Renwick. Is she at home?"

"No, suh."

"Do you know when she will return?"

"No, suh. She di'n' say. She took the day off from work."

"I see. Is Miss Webb in?"

The maid shook her head this time. "She's out, too, suh. I'm the only one in the house."

"I wonder when Miss Webb will return."

"She's gone shoppin'. It usually takes her hour or so."

"In that case I wonder if we might wait here until she returns."

The maid hesitated.

"I realize you people have been bothered lately by reporters and so forth, but if you care to check up on me I'm sure Miss Lowenstein at Miss Hira's office, or Mr. Howard Mantley—"

The maid brightened at once, flashing them a brief but wide-toothed smile. "You friend of Mr. Mantley? You come right in, suh!" Mr. Mantley never failed to give her a generous check at Christmas. She held the door wide, and they followed her ample back and buttocks down the hall to the drawing room.

"Jes' make yourselves at home, gentlemen. I'll tell Miss Francine, soon as she gits here." As an afterthought she added, "Is there anything I kin git you?"

Pierce opened his mouth, but Joseph answered swiftly, "Nothing, thank you."

The maid waddled off into the rear portions of the house, closing doors behind her as she went.

"Do you know Renwick well?" Joseph asked.

The reporter lowered his eyes to the piano keys. "No."

"I want you to stay here," said Joseph, "and play sentry while I have a look around. If anyone comes in the drive let out a whistle."

"Sure. What about the maid?"

"I doubt if she'll come back till Miss Webb arrives—unless someone comes to the front door."

"Okay. You might let me in on whatever you find."

"Certainly," agreed Joseph, having no intention of doing any such thing.

He left Pierce tinkling at the piano and walked down the main hall, glancing briefly in the den, library, hall closet, before he walked quickly and lightly up the stairs. Several bedrooms seemed to be closed off. They were furnished but looked unlived in. Ian's room, or what had evidently been his room, was a largish apartment with dressing room and bath, furnished in Empire style, but it had a deserted look. Mira's rooms, which adjoined, took up the rest of the front of the house. At the rear were the boy's smaller room with bunk beds, a desk, and workbench filled with model planes and ships, the usual boyish collection of useless, precious flotsam and jetsam, and a framed picture of Sean and his mother taken several years ago. Next to Sean's room he was surprised to find what must be Francine Webb's room. She was clearly treated as one of the family, not a servant or employee.

The room was bright and cheerful with yellow paper, rock maple furniture and ruffled blue organdy criss-cross curtains. The blue bedspread was nearly obliterated by a collection of sofa pillows, long-legged dolls and odd-looking stuffed animals. Her closet and drawers were neat and noncommittal. She used a light flowery scent. A small secretary in the window contained a good deal of blue notepaper. But blotter and pens were unused and dry. The bottle of black ink was full to the top. Miss Webb evidently did little correspondence. And if she kept any of the letters she received there was no sign of them. The room looked out over the rear yard and a swimming pool glinting greenly in the rain.

On an impulse he returned to the closet and searched it more thoroughly, being careful to put everything back exactly as he'd found it. At the rear, behind a long bag containing evening dresses, most of them quite old style, he found a battered portable typewriter. There was nothing else, however.

A microscopic bath opening off the cheerful bedroom yielded nothing unusual by way of drugs. Toothpaste, aspirin, gargle, eyewash, iodine and band-aids, bath powder, bubble-bath. Miss Webb evidently used few cosmetics; the lower shelf contained an all-purpose face cream, light pink face powder, a rose rouge and soft pink lipstick. Joseph closed the medicine cabinet and walked down the hall again to Mira's room.

Mira's desk was a business woman's desk even at home. Neatly stacked and filed bills—paid and unpaid. Correspondence, mostly social, awaiting reply. He had thought Mira the type of romantic woman who might keep a diary, but there was no sign of one here. The bedside table contained a few books, two modern best sellers, and a worn Robert Browning. The little drawer held a worn Bible.

The dressing room table offered him a bewildering assortment of expensive boxes and vials bearing the initials and names of leading cosmeticians—and nothing else.

Her bathroom cabinet duplicated Francine's except that there was more and a larger variety of everything. At the back he found a little flat prescription box of pheno-barbital with a Bel-Air Pharmacy label and a doctor's name, Candish, typed on the face. Joseph copied the names and serial number in his notebook.

Then on impulse he opened the towel cabinet adjoining the bathtub. Women, he knew, were quixotic creatures. They often read and even wrote in the bath. His probing hand reached beneath towels, soap boxes, toilet tissue and came up holding a small leather-bound book. It was not locked. There was a pencil stuck in the binding. He opened it to read, and a voice from the doorway said:

"Just what do you think you're doing in here?"

Joseph turned slowly to eye the boy framed in the open door. As he did so, he slipped the diary into his coat pocket.

"You're Sean Renwick, aren't you?"

"Who're you! And what are you doing in my mother's room?" There was annoyance and anger in the tone.

"You must have come up the back way," answered Joseph, unperturbed.

The boy nodded briefly. "I came up the service stairs to my room; then I heard something. I didn't see Emerald when I came in. Where's my mother? And where's Fran? And who are you?"

"One at a time," said Joseph. "Emerald, I take it, is the maid. She let Mr. Pierce and myself in some time ago. If you'd come in the front you'd have met him downstairs. We were making no effort to hide. When I left him he was playing the piano.

"Allow me to introduce myself. I'm Joseph Miles, a friend of your mother's. She seems to be out and so does Miss Webb, so I asked Emerald if we might wait until she comes."

"Who did you come to see?" asked the boy doubtfully.

"Either your mother or Miss Webb," lied Joseph. "But since your mother seems out for the day—"

"I think you're a pair of reporters," said Sean, narrowing his gray eyes. He was a stalwart, muscular lad, neat and trim in his gray school uniform. He was undeniably his father's son as far as appearances went, but something in his stance and voice and large capable hands reminded Joseph of his mother.

"I'm sorry if I made you uneasy," continued the Indian.

"I wasn't scared. I'm never scared!"

"I'm glad to hear that. When I was your age there was only one thing I was really afraid of—a wild stallion some boys and I had roped and corralled and hoped to break."

"A stallion?" The grey eyes widened a bit, and somehow the face lost its pinched, old look.

Joseph nodded. "I'm an Indian, you see. Nez Percé tribe. I was born on a reservation in Oregon. Horses were about the only sport we had as kids—"

"Gee!" All of boyhood's reluctant awe, admiration and envy were in that word.

"If you aren't familiar with the Oregon country, perhaps you would like me to tell you about it sometime."

"Sure thing! How about now?"

"Very well. But do you mind if in return I ask you a few things first?"

The boy was wary again but game.

"Okay."

"Aren't you supposed to be at school?"

Sean flushed and lowered his eyes. He looked more like Mira with his lashes down.

"Yeah, I guess so." Suddenly the lashes lifted and the candid gray eyes stared back at him defiantly. "But I came home anyway, because Mom's in trouble. She needs a man around. And I'm going to stay!"

"If that is the best way to help," said Joseph quietly, "I agree with you. I'm trying to help her myself."

"You are, honest?"

"Yes. Sean, if I let you in on a very personal secret, will you guarantee to keep it from everyone—except your mother?"

Sean nodded quickly. "Yeah. Sure I will, honest In—" He grinned suddenly, and Joseph grinned back.

"'Honest Injun' is a very good expression, Sean. So by all means let's use it in this case. As a matter of fact, I think we can help each other to free your mother from worry. You see, I happen to be a detective—a private investigator. I was called in on this case. But in order to function to the best of my ability, I am hoping to keep my profession a secret for the time being—from certain people."

"Gee! Are you really going to find out who killed Miss Lawrence?"

"I'm going to try—with your help."

"Honest, can I really help?"

"Certainly you can. Our conversations, of course, must remain secret for the time being. You understand?"

"Yeah!"

"Suppose you and I go somewhere where we can sit down undisturbed."

"Okay, Mr. Miles."

"Would you like to call me Joseph? It was my grandfather's name; he was a great chief in his day."

"Golly—sure." Sean was suddenly shy, darting out the door and through his mother's dressing room and bedroom.

"This way, Joseph," he whispered conspiratorially, leading off down the hall. He pushed open a baize-covered door onto a little landing. A steep flight of stairs led down to what must be a back hall.

"Come on up here." The boy slid open another door on the landing and they climbed dusty steps to a wide, only half-finished attic. The usual rubble, boxes, trunks piled and strewn about, but a small platform of boards under a tiny round window facing the drive had been fitted up as a boy's hideaway. A child's battered rolltop desk, a wobbly day bed, a chair, a bookcase of tattered favorites, portions of a dusty, dirty chemical set, an erector set and an electric train track filled most of the square.

"Sit down," whispered Sean, pounding an avalanche of dust out of the day bed cover in his enthusiasm.

Joseph coughed, used his handkerchief and sat down gingerly. Springs squeaked but held under him, and he relaxed. Sean perched beside him, knees drawn up to his chin, eyes sparkling with anticipation.

Speaking in his normal voice, Joseph said: "My friend below is to whistle when anyone comes. It would be better if neither Miss Webb nor the maid know that I've been upstairs."

Sean nodded. "I get it. Look, I'll stand by the window; you can see way down the hill from here. Then if I see a car or anybody you can get downstairs fast."

"A very good idea. The maid doesn't know you are at home?"

"Nope. She was probably in her room. She sits in there and listens to the radio whenever she gets a chance. She's lazy."

"Perhaps it's a good thing—for us. When I go downstairs I want you to go down the back way—unobserved if possible. Go outside and come to the front door as if you were just arriving. Is that clear?"

"Sure. I can do that easy."

"Splendid. Now—for the help you can give us. How long since you've seen your father?"

The gray eyes were lowered again. "Oh—Christmas, I guess."

"You haven't been home since then?"

"Oh, I've been home—mostly weekends. But he doesn't—I mean—"

"You are not fond of your father, are you?" Joseph helped him out.

"No, I guess not. He wasn't nice to my mother. Nobody likes him except a lot of crazy dames!" There was scorn in the youthful voice.

"I believe that on Tuesday, the day Miss Lawrence died, you phoned your mother?"

"I phoned to ask if I could go to Lake Tahoe with Freddie Benson over the weekend."

"What time did you phone?"

"Around one, I think. We'd had lunch. Fran said Mom wasn't home and for me not to bother her at the office; she said I could go unless Mother phoned that night to say I couldn't. I knew it was okay, though."

"It must be nice for you to have Miss Webb to call on when your mother is away."

"Yeah."

"She's always been with you?"

"Uh-huh. She's okay."

"I'm sure she is. Now I must ask you if you knew Miss Lawrence."

"I saw her in the movies, and she was here once or twice, but I only peeked in the window then."

"Did you know Mr. Vorman?"

Sean wrinkled his brow. "No."

"He was Miss Lawrence's manager. He was killed the other night, and there may be some connection."

"Oh."

"How about Mr. Mantley?"

The boy's face brightened. "I'll say! He gave me some ship models—from Sweden. They're swell! I'll show 'em—"

"Later, if you don't mind. Now tell me any of these women that you know or remember. Bonnie Bartlett—"

"She comes to see Mom sometimes. She's funny. She smokes Egyptian cigarettes."

"She does? Miss Lowenstein—Jessica—"

"Sure, she works at Mom's. She's okay."

"And Alma Roberts?"

"No."

"She's your mother's secretary." Then Joseph asked, "How about Maggie Tally?"

Again Sean's face brightened. "Yeah. She's been here a lot of times; she sews for Mom. When I was real little she made me a cowboy suit. It had real leather chaps, too."

"Was Miss Tally here one day when you quarreled with your father?"

Sean flushed furiously and told his first downright lie. "I don't remember."

Joseph went on smoothly with his next question. "Know Mr. Duke Rossi?"

"No, I don't."

"Thank you, Sean. Now tell me, when you come home as you did today, secretly, how do you get inside? Do you have a key?"

"No." The boy looked suddenly mischievous and conspiratorial. "There's a loose board on the basement window. I can open the catch with a stick. It's over the washtrays, so it's easy to crawl down."

Joseph smiled back. Suddenly a sharp, cautious whistle rose faintly from the lower region.

Sean, eyes glued to the window, yelped, "Golly! It's Fran—she's coming fast, too! You'd better—"

Joseph was on his feet, moving carefully across the square of planks. "Go down the back way," he told the boy.

Sean nodded vigorously.

"And be sure to brush some of that dust off before you come in the front."

Sean laughed as he watched the Indian disappear silently down the stairs. A moment later he darted after him like a rabbit down a hole.

CHAPTER XI

Mira ignored the rap on the door.

"Hey—you in there?"

It was a new voice, one she had never heard before.

"Yes—what do you want?" She forced her voice to be haughty, cool.

"The boss says to tell you your car's outside. It's okay now. Full of gas. She was bone dry. You can go."

"Leave here?" breathed Mira. "I can go? Now?"

"Yeah, sure. Your car's waitin', lady."

She scrambled madly from the bed, began to get into her dry wrinkled clothes while talking to herself like a madwoman.

"I'll make him pay!" was all she could recall clearly afterwards. "I'll make him pay for scaring me!"

Joseph and Pierce were still at Mira's when she returned home.

Joseph explained to Pierce that he would get much more out of Mira by himself, and the reporter grudgingly agreed to wait outside in the Ford while Joseph waited to see her after she was settled down in bed.

"Tell me," said Joseph later, seated next to Mira's bed, "exactly what happened."

Mira told him, omitting nothing except Duke Rossi's personal behavior. She even told him of her suspicion of Rossi.

"I have had the same idea," said Joseph. "After all, he had cocktails with her, his men brought up sealed bottles, he could have had opportunity and motive."

"And yet," said Mira, "why should he desire her death?"

"She might have had something on him."

"Duke Rossi has nothing to hide," said Mira firmly, "and he wouldn't care about the rest of the world knowing, if he did have."

"Perhaps not. He's a strange person."

Mira took a handkerchief from her satin bedjacket pocket. "Must you go on with this, Mr. Miles? I'm very tired."

"I must. Sorry. Tell me about the night Vorman died. Is there anything you might add to what you told the police?"

Mira held herself in check, and then suddenly she began to speak the truth, almost as if something inside her were prodding her on against her will.

"Edgar wanted to meet me because he had something to say. He wasn't that way as a rule. I mean he didn't believe in letting you in on anything."

"So you think it was something very special?"

"Yes."

Mira opened her bed-table drawer and gave him the bookmatches and cigarettes and coin keyring she had taken from Edgar Vorman's pocket.

"These may be important." She told him how she had gotten them.

"Yes, thank you." He turned the keyring in his dark fingers. "Does this mean anything to you?"

"No. I've never seen it before. It's an old coin or medallion made into a keyring, isn't it?"

"I should say so. You don't know if it belonged to Mr. Vorman?"

"I don't; I'm sorry. I didn't know him particularly well."

"Perhaps your husband might know."

"Ian? I doubt it. Vorman wasn't his friend." She colored slightly and looked out of the window.

Joseph put the coin in his pocket and changed the subject. "You have an exceedingly bright son, Miss Mira."

Mira smiled. "Thank you. We think so, of course. I'm afraid Fran and I have spoiled him."

"His father didn't?"

"No. I'm afraid Sean and his father never really understood each other very well. It is unfortunate."

"I'm going to ask you some very personal questions, Miss Hira, only because I think that they are pertinent to your safety. You realize now that someone desires your death?"

Mira's face whitened as she lowered her lashes. "Yes."

"I want to know the terms of your will, if you have made one."

She glanced up quickly, obviously startled. "My will? Yes, I made one when we moved here some years ago. Then I changed a few things when Ian and I separated. It will probably have to be changed again after our property settlement and divorce."

"How was your property left in the first will?"

"The bulk of it to Ian, during his life, and then to Sean, providing Ian didn't re-marry. His own will was the same. Ian only had a small income, but has expectations from abroad."

The Indian nodded.

"Then I had a few personal bequests to my employees."

"May I ask what they were? All of this may be important."

Mira frowned in concentration. "There's a ten-thousand-dollar trust fund for Fran, five thousand each for Jessica and Maggie—they've all been with me for years—provided they are in my employ at the time of decease."

"And the business?"

"Jointly to Ian and Jessica, because he could never run it by himself. It's community property under California law, but Ian had agreed to the arrangement."

"I see. And what changes did you make recently on your separation?"

"I cut Ian out of my will—after the property settlement. I figured my personal money should go elsewhere. Everything went to Sean, in trust, with my lawyer as executor. And I increased the bequests to the others by one thousand dollars each. That's all."

The Indian rose, standing tall and erect, his dark enigmatic face turned toward her. "I'm going to speak very plainly again, Miss Hira. This whole thing is still a puzzle to me, as I believe it is to my colleagues, Reame and Greene, but there is one point upon which we all agree—your personal danger. That is why I want you to promise me that you will not leave the house until I give you permission."

"But the shop—"

"I spoke with Miss Lowenstein today," smiled Joseph. "She strikes me as a highly competent young woman."

"Yes, she is. I suppose I could do part of my work by phone."

"Do so by all means. I would suggest also that you keep your son here at home for a while."

Mira sat up stiffly, her cheeks as white as paper, her dark blue eyes enormous in her suddenly drawn face. "Mr. Miles, you don't think Sean is in danger?"

"I'm not sure, but I don't want to take any chances. It won't hurt to keep the boy here for a few days."

"No, of course not. And I thank you for everything." She smiled wanly up at him and held out her hand. He took it solemnly and shook it.

"I'm going to ask you one last favor, Miss Hira. I want to pay a visit to your husband. Would you object if I took Sean with me?"

"No, of course I don't object. His father wanted to see him this week anyway."

"Any special reason?"

"No, I don't believe so. He gets these fatherly streaks." She smiled. "I imagine this one was brought on because I told him I was going ahead with the divorce, and Ian doesn't want the divorce."

"Could it be that he is still in love with you?"

"I don't know. Ian was always too deep and complex for me. He says he is, but—" Mira's voice trailed off.

"And may I ask if you are still in love with him?"

Mira hesitated this time, opening her hands and staring into the square palms as if she could read her future there.

"I'm not sure. I was, until last night—"

"And then?"

"Something, I don't know what, changed when he kissed me in the tea house." She saw the pitfall the moment she had spoken and a little gasp escaped her lips.

"Your husband met you in the tea house?"

"Yes." It was a whisper, a mere thread of sound. Then in a rush she added, "He came quite by accident—to get some air. Ian always does that when the air at a party gets too stuffy. He has a bronchial condition. I was there to meet Edgar—Ian only stayed a moment. I didn't tell him why I was there."

"However, he could have hung about watching and listening, Miss Hira. And when he saw who it was—"

"No!" she cried. "He didn't, he wouldn't!" She put her hands over her face and began to sob.

Joseph's voice continued woodenly. "I must speak for your own good, Miss Hira. You should have told this to the police. Do you know anything else that you are concealing?"

She shook her head miserably and leaned back against the pillows, completely spent.

Pierce dumped his passengers at the entry of the Saracen Arms and drove off with a clashing of worn gears.

Sean and Joseph walked through the black and chromium lobby, passed an empty glass-brick reception desk, and entered an elaborate self-service elevator, padded in white leather. Sean gaily operated the elevator and directed Joseph to his father's apartment.

The door was black also—some highly polished wood with a chromium number, and a small card in a chromium-edged plate with Renwick's name engraved on it. Before the bell had finished pealing from Sean's first jab, the door was opened by a thin, scared-looking Chinese boy. He wore a tan and blue sports coat and tan slacks.

"Yes?"

Joseph opened his mouth to reply, but Sean forestalled him.

"Where's Dad?"

A voice inside the apartment exclaimed sharply, and Ian's tall, blue dressing-gowned figure replaced the Chinese at the door, moving him aside.

"Sean! By Jove! Come in, my lad." One hand held a glass; he put the other about the boy's shoulders as if to draw him close, but Sean squirmed away. Ian Renwick's eyes narrowed perceptibly, and then he seemed conscious of Joseph's presence for the first time.

"You were at Mantley's last night," he said levelly. "Friend of Rossi's or something? I won't ask now what you're doing with my boy; come in."

Joseph followed father and son into a large, ultramodern living room and sat down on the nearest chair. It was surprisingly comfortable despite its tortuous shape.

Ian pulled the boy onto a scarlet couch by his side and motioned to the standing Chinese. "Fix a drink, Billy. For both of you. How about you, sport?" He turned to Sean. "Care for a ginger ale, or coca cola?"

"All right," said Sean. "Coke, I guess."

The Chinese served the drinks with a wary eye and shaking hands.

Ian turned to Joseph. "May I ask for an explanation now?"

"Yes," replied the Indian, crossing his legs. "Mr. Rossi and Mr. Mantley are both friends of mine. Naturally I am interested in what happened last night at the Mantley party. I would like to compare notes with you—as a bystander."

"Why me? Who are you? What do you want?"

"The truth, Mr. Renwick. I know that you were with Miss Lawrence the night she died."

"I didn't kill her! Heaven knows I wished her dead—but I didn't kill her. Where would I get morphine?"

"It's rather simple to obtain—in certain cases. It may have been served in one of your drinks."

"I tell you I didn't—wait, was there any trace in a glass, a container?"

"No. But it's possible to scour them sufficiently."

"There were only four cups. You think one of them—"

"No. The police found them all innocent."

"Then—"

"There's a chance they were used and cleansed."

"You theorize a good deal."

"Yes."

"And Vorman? What about him?"

"A cement walk leaves no footprints. The butler claims no one uninvited entered. The rock used was rough lava and left no prints."

"And how do you know all this, Mr. Miles?" Renwick's voice grew nasty. "I'll tell you! You're a common, filthy little 'tec', hoping, like a hyena, to feast off someone else's kill!"

Joseph, ignoring him, turned to address the Chinese boy. "Aren't you Billy Wong, an employee of Miss Hira's?"

He nodded swiftly.

"What difference does that make!" roared Ian. "Leave him alone!"

Joseph held the eyes of the Chinese. "You mixed and carried Mr. Renwick's drinks the day Miss Lawrence died. Was there any moment at which he or anyone else could have tampered with the drinks?"

Billy Wong shook his head vigorously. "No, no! I just took them up and left them. I don't know after that. I went."

Joseph sat back and rested his head against the chair. "If it wasn't you, Renwick, or your wife or Mr. Rossi—we have rather a wide field left anyway. Mr. Vorman is dead. There's Miss Bartlett—by a wide stretch she could have done it according to the medical examiners. Or any of you could have returned and given Miss Lawrence the poison while she was in a semicomatose state."

"And just how did we all get in? The tower room was locked."

"Your wife was alone, asleep, in her office. She had a pass-key on her desk. Anyone could have taken it."

"I assure you," said Renwick seriously, "I did not."

"I believe you, because it would have been too simple for you to get a duplicate from your wife at any time. You may have always had one."

Joseph got up, hands in his pockets. "I wonder if you could tell me if Miss Lawrence kept a maid?"

"No," said Renwick. "Not that I know of. Oh, there was an ex-dresser of hers used to work for her now and then."

"Do you recall her name?"

"No. It was Almarina something—"

"I'll see you later, if I may, Mr. Renwick?"

Renwick said nothing as the Chinese boy went to open the door.

Sean refused to say goodbye to his father, and Joseph led him reluctantly down to a taxi, put the boy inside, and directed it to Mira's home.

He went back and entered the phone booth in the Saracen lobby and phoned the service employment bureaus. On the tenth call he learned that an Almarina V. Bagley was now employed by Miss Bonnie Bartlett at 1518 Mandeville Canyon.

Bonnie Bartlett's house was a small, low, square white brick affair with a tile roof.

The door chimes brought a hefty, red-faced maid of middle age, dressed in a tight-fitting black uniform.

"Yes?" she asked warily. Her gray hair was done in a tight bun; her sharp black eyes were suspicious between narrow lids.

"Is Miss Bartlett at home?" asked Joseph.

"No."

"I'm a friend of hers."

"From the studios?" The voice was bitter.

"No. I want to help her on the Mantley business."

The door opened slowly. "Come in. She might want to see you. She's gone swimming down the road. You can wait if you like."

Joseph followed her through a small neat hall into a restricted living room, with a dining table at one end. This was not his idea of the residence of a successful movie star. He wondered what she did with her large salary. Investments? Did she support a family some-where—a host of clinging relations? He doubted it.

It was a small lot. The house he judged to be five rooms at the most, hardly more than a cottage. The furnishings were attractive—rock maple and gay chintz—but obviously inexpensive reproductions, not antiques.

The maid motioned him to a seat and turned abruptly to leave.

"It was a terribly upsetting business for everyone," said Joseph in a light bantering way. "I was there, too, I've picked up a few details about the investigation and thought I'd pass them on to Bonnie." He hoped she would think him an intimate friend of the actress.

"If you're in pictures you know how it is," shrugged the woman. "I've been around stage folks all my life, and I know there's one thing they can't stand, and that's scandal."

"Right," drawled Joseph, stretching out his legs and leaning back in his chair indolently. "Was it really as bad in the old days?"

Almarina patted a cushion and straightened an ashtray. "It was worse. One breath of scandal and you were done." She laughed harsh-ly. "Maybe I just missed this by the skin of my teeth. I used to be her dresser."

"Whose?"

"Floren Lawrence."

"No! Tell me about it." He pulled out his case and brought it across to her. The suspicion slowly died out of her eyes as she perched on the edge of a couch.

"Don't mind if I do. Thanks. Bonnie smokes them Egyptian things. Awful! Why anyone who can buy good American tobacco wants those foreign things— But a lot of actresses are nuts about anything foreign. Think it's glamorous, I guess."

She puffed her cigarette, squinting up her eyes against the smoke. "I don't go to the pictures now—sick of 'em. But I think I've seen you somewheres. Been at it long?"

"Long enough."

She nodded.

"What was Floren like?" he asked suddenly, taking a seat across from her in a maple rocker.

"She was all right most of the time. Had her quirks and moods like all of 'em. She was man-crazy and lived by the main chance. But don't we all?"

"Why did you leave her?"

"Oh, same reason. She and Bonnie were sharing her apartment, and I thought Bonnie knew better where she was goin' and would get there quicker."

Joseph nodded and glanced idly about the room, noting the absence of books or magazines, barring a few motion picture monthlies and copies of *Variety*.

"Doesn't look like Bonnie reads any more than Floren." He smiled.

Almarina sat back and crossed her plump legs with an effort. "That's where you're wrong, young man. Bonnie don't read a thing but *Variety* and them movie magazines. But Floren used to read all the time, everything she could get her hands on. She'd come home from a late party and sit in bed readin' till five or six in the morning. She always had some book or clipping in her bag to read on the set or wherever she was during the day.

"She loved the newspapers; had a lot of newspaper friends. I think her old man was a reporter in Chicago. Anyway, she had a bunch of out-of-town papers sent to her every week. She'd read 'em all, too! Once in a while if she was too busy she'd skim through 'em and mark parts for me to cut out so she could take 'em along to read more carefully later on. Oh, she was always readin'. And was she a sucker for every visitin' reporter that come to town! She'd always fall for a hard luck story. Sometimes I got to thinkin' she did it for an investment. Good press relations are worth a mint to a star, ain't they?"

"Yes," agreed Joseph dreamily, "they sure are." Suddenly he glanced at his wristwatch and jumped up with an exclamation. "I can't wait any longer; got an appointment with my agent." He looked around for his hat, picked it up and came back to the startled maid. "Tell Bonnie I'll phone her later. I enjoyed the talk. Goodbye."

"Wait—Mr.—who shall I say called?"

But Joseph was already closing the door, and by the time she pulled it open again his cab was rolling down the road under the tall trees.

CHAPTER XII

At closing time Maggie Tally put on her tweed coat, old felt hat, and searched for an empty paper sack to bundle her black work apron up in. She always took them home to launder herself. She got a clean paper bag from the workroom supply closet and began to remove the items from the two apron pockets. In her own work table drawer she neatly arranged her scissors, the fat red pincushion full of sharp wicked-looking pins, a piece of dressmaker's chalk, her tape measure, a stub of pencil, a soiled handkerchief, two thimbles, and a shred of tweed material. That was odd, because they hadn't had any tweed material in the shop in ages. It looked old, too, and worn. It wasn't the color of her own coat, which was a greenish beige. The scrap—if you could call it that—more like a shred of raveling—was grey and black with a touch of red. More like a man's tweed, she thought.

She went to the big wastebasket and stopped to put it on top of the day's huge pile of scraps and snippings. One of the seamstresses coming in from the lavatory heard Maggie muttering something about the janitor.

"He'll clear all that out tonight," she said brightly, standing in front of a mirror to put on her hat. Suddenly she saw Maggie stiffen behind her. Maggie's hand went out to the wastebasket, the girl was to tell later, and snatched up a scrap to put it in her coat pocket. Then she turned abruptly, leaving her apron half rolled up on the table, and went quickly out of the room. She didn't return.

Maggie, her felt hat slightly askew, burst into Mira's office, startling Alma and Jessica who were conversing in low tones at Alma's desk.

"Good heavens, Maggie," Jessica laughed, "you scared us half to death! The place isn't on fire, is it?"

Maggie fell back, suddenly flustered and red-faced. "No, of course not. I mean—I just wanted to see Miss Hira—"

"But you know she's not here today," said Jessica. She exchanged glances with Alma, who was watching the seamstress avidly. "Don't you feel well, Maggie? Is something wrong?"

"Certainly not!" Maggie was indignant now and defensive. "I just had something to tell her. That is," Maggie wet her lips and tried desperately to remain calm, "I wanted to show her something, and ask her if I should tell that nice newspaper man who interviewed me. He said if I thought of anything else—"

Jessica came from the desk and put her arm about the elder woman's shoulders. "Maggie, you are not making sense at all. Mira isn't in any condition to be bothered, unless it's vitally important. Now just what is it you want to say to her?"

"I only want to tell *her*—first," said Maggie stubbornly. "She'll decide if I should tell that nice newspaper man—"

"We've had enough of that, I should think!" snapped Alma.

Jessica withdrew her arm and shrugged her slim shoulders. "I can't have you bothering Mira right now. But if it's really so important to you, you can put it in a note and I'll take it to Mira tonight when I go up to see her. I have some things to go over with her anyway."

Maggie seemed torn by indecision.

"You can go in there and write," said Alma, nodding toward Mira's office. Suddenly Maggie turned and bolted inside, slamming the door behind her.

"Now I ask you," wailed Alma.

Jessica stood frowning at the closed door. Presently it opened and Maggie thrust a sealed envelope into Jessica's hand. "You'll see she gets it?"

"Yes."

Maggie nodded and walked out. . . .

Maggie let herself in her warm, cheerfully lighted house and shivered. It was so open, so vulnerable alone like this between empty lots, and with the shades up.

She went through the house, pulling down all the shades, making sure windows and doors were fastened. It was silly, she told herself, very silly to be afraid. Nicky, the cat, was curled up asleep on his footstool, purring faintly. She was glad he was a young cat.

She went to the bedroom and turned down the bed, laid her nightgown on the foot and went back to the closet. She felt in her work-coat pocket and brought out the shred of tweed. Glancing about the room, she picked up first a jewel box decorated with sea shells, then rummaged in a dresser drawer for a handkerchief case, putting it back in favor of a stocking box. Then she abandoned them all and went back to the parlor.

Nicky opened one eye and watched lazily while she hid the scrap of tweed in the safest spot she could imagine, and turned flushed with triumph to scratch his ears.

"Now Mother can go to bed and read a nice book. But first, you have to go out. Come along." She picked up the big cat and, taking him back to the kitchen, shoved him out.

She was in the bathroom creaming her face before the cloudy mirror and listening to the maddening tap of dripping water in the tub when her ears recorded another alien sound. A board creaked once, loudly, on the porch. She knew exactly where that board was, on her side, near the front door. It always creaked when someone stepped on it. Not a cat or a dog, but a person. For an instant she stood frozen and stiff, staring into her own wide eyes in the mirror. It was like looking at an eerie stranger from another planet. The face shiny and distorted by the cream and the wavy mirror, the mouth slack, the eyes—she had never seen herself looking frightened before. The mantel clock began to strike nine dully. When it had finished the knocking began on the front door.

Maggie crept forward and peered out into the dimly lit hall. She could see an outline through the frosted glass panel. Then a familiar voice said: "Are you there? It's only me."

Relief flooded through her like a tidal wave, leaving her weak and giddy. She stumbled to the door with a glad little cry. Reaching out, she flung the door wide on its hinges. . . .

CHAPTER XIII

Greene, Reame and Joseph drove up to Floren's apartment on Canon Drive. It was in a Moorish-façaded building shaded by whispering banana palms and weeping willows. There were four flats, one to a floor. Floren's was at the top. Most of the apartment house was dark.

"Is this the same apartment she shared with Bonnie Bartlett?" asked Joseph as they stood in a high-beamed room furnished in heavy, carved Spanish furniture.

Reame nodded. He stood under a wrought iron chandelier and pointed. "Bedrooms over there—two of 'em. Bath between. Kitchen back there, next to the dining room. Den over here." He turned toward the opposite wall and started across the thick Sarouk toward a partly opened paneled door with a wrought iron ring instead of a knob.

They all saw it at the same time. The only light they had put on was the big three-tiered chandelier that Reame had flicked on as he entered from the hall. But a faint gleam of light was coming from the den through the partly opened door.

With an exclamation Reame leaped for the threshold and swung the door back with a slam. All three crowded through the opening. A pocket flashlight lying on the carpet spewed light over Bonnie Bartlett's body sprawled ungratefully near a bookcase. On hands and knees, leaning over her, was Duke Rossi, his face as hard as chiseled steel, a heavy bronze paperweight in his gloved right hand.

Reame leaped forward, knocking him off balance, and kicked the paperweight savagely out of his hand. Rossi gathered himself quickly, murderous hatred in his dark eyes, but Reame flashed a gun, growling, "Hold it, Rossi. You're covered."

Joseph and Greene bent to examine the girl. The back of her head felt soft but the only blood came from her nose. She opened her eyes for a moment, smiled at them and closed them again.

"Fracture or concussion," said Greene. He got up and used the telephone, calling four numbers in rapid succession.

They covered Bonnie with blankets and went to wait in the next room. Duke Rossi sat sullenly on a sofa rubbing the hand Reame had kicked.

"Okay," Reame said. "Want to talk—or save it for later?"

Rossi looked up at Joseph. "I didn't do it."

"How do you happen to be here?" asked the Indian softly.

"I got home from San Pedro this afternoon."

"We know about that, too," rasped Reame.

"Go on," said Joseph.

"Well, I went out to some friends' for a swim. I met Bonnie there. She asked me to stop by her place for a drink. When we got there the maid was kinda upset over somethin'—she and Bonnie go into a huddle. Pretty soon Bonnie asks me to drive her over here. Says she's gotta get some stuff."

"She had a key, I suppose? Or did you pick the lock?"

"She had a key. She useta live here."

"And you thought it was okay for her to come bargin' in here like that when Miss Lawrence had just been murdered? You came in with her—"

"No, I didn't. She wouldn't let me. Asked me to wait. Said she'd be about twenty minutes."

"And—"

"I waited. When she didn't come out after twenty-five minutes I came up. The door was unlatched, so I came in and found her—like that. Then you guys got here."

"Very neat!" said Reame, "and not worth a plugged nickel! We've got you, but good, this time, Rossi."

Rossi looked ugly.

"Do you mind if I speak to him alone?" asked Joseph.

"It can't do any harm." Greene smiled. "It's all grist for the mill. Go ahead, Joe; the Beverly boys'll be here in a minute."

"Now look here, Greene!" Reame protested.

"You want to crack this case as soon as possible, don't you?" snapped the other. He jerked his head toward the Indian. "Let 'em talk."

Joseph touched Rossi's arm.

They walked across the room to the nearest bedroom. Joseph closed the door and indicated the bed. They sat side by side on top of the green satin spread and Joseph got out cigarettes. The furniture was dark and heavy like the living room. A glass-topped dressing table contained a battery of giant-sized perfume bottles.

"I've gotta get in touch with my lawyer," Rossi began. "They'll try to railroad me."

"You've no idea who attacked Bonnie?"

The other shook his head.

"You didn't see anyone come into the building while you sat outside?"

"Nope. The place was a morgue. I think Bonnie said two apartments are empty anyway."

"Then someone may already have been here—waiting for her."

"Yeah, I never thought of that."

"You were very opportune in rescuing Mira Hira today," said Joseph. "Have you any ideas about what happened?"

Rossi jerked his head up as if he had been thinking of something else. "Somebody'd drained off most of her gas, I'd say. And there were a couple of loose wires, that could or couldn't have been done on purpose."

Outside in the living room they heard the doorbell ring, then the opening of the front door and the tramp of feet on the floor.

"Looks like it's begun," sighed Rossi. He turned to Joseph. "You're still workin' for me?"

The Indian nodded. "I don't believe you did this, Mr. Rossi. You don't quite fill the tracks I'm following."

"Thanks, pal." Rossi got up and stretched; for an instant a wry smile touched his lips. "You're okay. So's Mira Hira. Look out for her, will yuh, pal?"

"Yes."

The door behind him opened and Greene and Reame came in.

"I'm taking you in, Rossi," said the latter.

Greene told Joseph, "They've taken the girl to the hospital—she's still alive. They're going to keep us posted."

"Still want to look through Lawrence's papers?" asked Greene. Joseph nodded.

"Come on then. The boys are working in there, but I don't think we'll get in their way."

Photographers and fingerprint men were working swiftly and efficiently in the den when they went in. Greene, stepping over a flash bulb on the rug, indicated the bottom two rows of a built-in bookcase. They were filled to the top with neatly folded newspapers.

"This could be an all-night job," he grumbled, getting down on his haunches.

Joseph knelt down and pulled out a few papers at random, fingering through them. He turned to Greene. "Did she have a scrap-book, or press-book, anything in which she kept notes or pictures?"

"I don't think so."

Joseph got up and began to examine the books on the shelves, volume by volume.

When he found something several hours later he was alone in the apartment and it was not what he had expected.

A plain white business-size envelope, sealed and with the word "Clips" printed in ink on the front, had been shoved inside a tooled leather book cover on a Thesaurus. Not many people would dally long with a Thesaurus, not Floren Lawrence's friends at least. It was a safe hiding place.

Turning on the desk lamp, he sat down and slit the envelope with a bronze paper knife, evidently the companion piece to the paper weight that had been used as a weapon.

There were a good many clippings, some yellow with age, some quite new. All had the date and source written in red pencil across the top.

Joseph was puzzled by the subject matter. Some of them, it was true, contained juicy bits concerning celebrities taken from the gossip columns. But there were also announcements of births, deaths, marriages and divorces, fashion reports, horse race results, and one or two clippings about Floren's pictures.

He began, with a sigh, to read each one carefully. When he had finished them there still seemed nothing incriminating in the clips. Of course he didn't know all the people mentioned, and one of the people he was interested in could very well be masquerading as different personalities. But none of the salient facts seemed to fit.

He examined the envelope again—shook it out on the blotter. A fragment of paper fluttered down and lay still. The writing was minute but it was undeniably Floren's.

"Taking Chi. Nov 5th 1937 to Mira."

Joseph got up and put the clipping and envelope in his breast pocket. The scrap of paper he put carefully in his wallet. Then the phone rang.

"Yes?" He kept his voice as ordinary as possible.

"Mr. Miles?"

"Yes, Miss Hira. How did you—"

"Thank heaven you're there! Fran has taken Sean to the movies, and I'm alone here with Emerald. Duke Rossi has been arrested—his lawyer just phoned me. He said you were there, at Floren's. I want to help—won't you please come up here?"

Joseph glanced at his watch. It was 9:05.

"Yes," he told her. "I'll be right there."

"Thank you." Mira rang off.

Joseph dismissed the taxi a little below the house and walked the remainder of the way, on softly moving Indian feet.

Emerald answered the door, but Mira was right in back of her, in a lime green wool dress and green leather sandals.

"Thank heaven you're here!" She pulled Joseph into the den and shut the door. She looked weary, ill and frightened.

At her motion Joseph sat beside her on a leather window seat.

"It's awful, awful! I don't think for a moment Duke—Mr. Rossi—attacked Bonnie. Do you, Mr. Miles?"

"I'm not sure," said Joseph cautiously, "but I doubt it."

She let out her breath with a sigh. "You'll do something about it?"

"I'm trying to find the murderer, yes."

Mira laughed suddenly. "Everyone's trying to do that. Even my employees. Jessica brought up my mail and then left on a secret mission of her own; she seems to think she knows where the morphine came from."

"That is very interesting," replied the Indian, his face impassive, his black eyes narrowed to slit.

"And," rattled on Mira restlessly, "my seamstress, Maggie Tally, sent me the most absurd note. Jessica says she thinks old maids like Maggie can't take this sort of strain for long."

"What was in the note?"

"Oh, a lot of gibberish about finding something on the hall floor of the tower the night Floren died."

Joseph sat stiffly in his chair; not a muscle moved to betray his excitement, but his eyes took on a reddish gleam.

"I must ask to know exactly what was in that note, Miss Hira. Where is it?"

"Oh, I threw it in the fire with the other mail odds and ends when Jessica left."

"Did she know its contents?"

"Why, of course! We read it together and laughed over it."

"Then you must tell me as much as you remember. I cannot stress the importance too much."

Mira looked startled and uneasy. She knit her hands in her lap and began, "Well, she said she wondered if I wanted her to give additional information to the papers, and that she'd forgotten all about picking up something on the hall rug at the tower the night Floren died. She said it was a piece of tweed and that she was certain it was not off of any material in our shop."

"Did she say what she'd done with it?"

"No."

"Has she a phone?"

"No, I don't believe she has."

Joseph got up and reached for the desk phone. He dialed his hotel. "Any messages? Mr. Miles. Thank you." He replaced the receiver slowly.

"She tried to call me. I'd posed as a reporter at your place today."

"You?"

"Yes. It's vital that I get to Miss Tally at once."

"I'll drive you," said Mira. "Wait till I get my coat and keys."

She was back in four minutes. They went out through the kitchen, where Mira spoke briefly to a drowsy, sullen Emerald, and then Joseph opened the garage doors while Mira backed her car out. As they drove off, it was 9:30 by Joseph's watch.

It was 10:17 when Mira pulled to a stop beside the quiet, dark duplex. Joseph rapped loudly on both doors and got no response. At his third sally a huge white Persian cat came around the left of the house and mewed mournfully.

"This must be Nicky," said Mira, picking the cat up. "She always talked about him; he was all she had. But why am I talking like this! Can't you break in the door? I'm scared." She shivered.

Joseph, without replying, went round to the back with Mira at his heels. He touched the French doors and they fell open. The cat leaped out of Mira's arms and bounded inside. Joseph touched a wall switch, and the small light over the breakfast nook went on.

"Stay here," he told Mira flatly.

"No! Let me go with you."

"Very well." He crossed the room and entered the hall, turning on lights as he found them, peering into rooms briefly.

From the front of the house came a sharp cry, a dreadful snarl and hissing.

Joseph ran forward, followed by Mira. He turned on the lights from the switch by the door, and the neat little parlor sprang into view.

Mira cried out, pressing a hand over her mouth.

Joseph bent down over the still form by the fireplace. The cat continued to arch his back and hiss in a corner.

"Is she—?" began Mira piteously.

"Yes, Miss Hira. Dead. Her skull has been crushed—with that, I imagine." He glanced toward a heavy iron poker on the hearth, dulled with blood and hair.

Mira began to cry. "She was such a good woman. So loyal, and so faithful! I loved her—"

"I'm very sorry—about everything," said the Indian. "But I must phone the police. Will you come and wait in the car?"

She nodded miserably and followed him out the back way to the car they had parked at the curb.

CHAPTER XIV

Leaving Mira huddled down in the seat of the car, the Indian made his way back inside the house to await the Santa Monica police.

He went silently and systematically through the little apartment, noting the unhidden signs of a more hurried former search. There was a chance, a slim one, that Maggie's cache had eluded the searcher. He left the obvious places till last. Women, he had found, seldom employ the obvious or conventional if another approach is available. He searched the kitchen, the bathroom and bedroom in order, and found nothing. He had firm faith in his powers as a searcher. Therefore he reached the conclusion that the hidden scrap of tweed must be in the parlor. Avoiding the sprawled form and the dying fire, he lifted flower pots, peered under table ledges, dug a finger into the peat moss of a hanging basket. As a last resort he climbed on a straight chair and looked behind an oval mirror hanging above the mantel.

Nothing.

He was replacing the mirror when the sound of sirens startled him and he jerked back, half-slipping off the chair, and righted himself on a small, sturdy oak table holding a fat goldfish bowl. The table held, though Joseph found himself momentarily with his nose hovering two inches above the lurching water and fish. In the depths he was conscious of something long and dark that lay very still. A dead fish? A piece of that seaweed stuff they float in goldfish bowls?

Getting off the chair, he reached out and lifted the bowl in both hands. Underneath was a hand-crocheted doily; on top of the doily was the unmistakable shred of tweed. Joseph juggled the fishbowl to one arm and picked up his find, then put the bowl back on the doily.

He grinned fleetingly, and his obsidian eyes took on a reddish glow. It was exactly where Maggie Tally would hide something, and not bad, at that. How many people ever stare down directly into a goldfish bowl, unless they are feeding the fish? They usually watch from the sides.

The sirens were dying outside, and in two minutes the same young detective inspector and sergeant whom Joseph had met at Mantley's strode in.

"Lord!" said the Inspector. "We're having our share of this stuff. What do you make of it?"

Joseph told them everything that had happened that night, omitting only his private talk with Rossi, and the finding of the things at Floren's and the tweed scrap here. He felt that things would move faster if he passed them on to Greene.

"I did search the place," he added. "I realize I've over-stepped my rights—"

"Oh," said the young Inspector, "that's okay. We'll watch for your prints."

"I might say that whoever did this must have been a friend or at least an acquaintance of the deceased."

"Yeah?"

Joseph nodded. "She obviously opened the door herself, unhesitatingly, although she was alone here, without even her neighbors present, and in a reportedly highly nervous state. As you can see, she was ready to retire. Certainly under the circumstances she would not have admitted a casual caller."

"No, I guess not. Still, dames are screwy, especially old ones like this."

Joseph, reserving comment, rose. "If you're through with me, I will drive Miss Hira home. She is in no condition to stay here."

"Sure," agreed the inspector. "You go ahead, Miles. We'll call you if we want something else."

Outside, Joseph found Mira with her head thrown back against the car seat but with her eyes wide open and staring fixedly into space.

He opened the door on the opposite side and got behind the wheel.

"I'm taking you home," he said softly.

She did not reply.

The big house atop the hill in Bel Air was quiet and solemn as they braked to a stop before the front door.

If the detective was still watching from the garage he was well hidden.

Mira used her latchkey, and in the front hall's dim light Joseph saw that his watch said 11:35.

Mira led him resolutely through swinging doors to the spacious kitchen.

"You may as well see where we spend most of our time," she said over one shoulder. "Here, make yourself useful." She got out whiskey, soda water, glasses, and pointed to the oversize refrigerator. "Ice in there. I'll see about sandwiches."

She was slicing French bread when Emerald, arrayed in a black and green satin robe, looked in sleepily from the back hall.

"'At you, Miz Hira?"

"Yes, Emerald. You needn't bother. Did Sean and Miss Fran get in from the show?"

"Uh-huh. 'Bout twenty minutes ago."

"Oh, so late? Must have gone to a preview show."

"I think so, Miz Hira. They both say not wake 'em so early in the mo'nin', they goin' to sleep."

"All right, Emerald, thank you. We'll all sleep late."

The Negress closed the door and padded off down the back hall.

The front doorbell rang briefly.

"Who on earth—" began Mira, going to the door.

Jessica, her hair disheveled and her dark eyes wide with fright, stood swaying on the threshold. "I know," she mumbled. "I know who did it! Mira—"

The Indian, pushing Mira aside, took the other girl's arm and led her gently but firmly into the house. He put her in the nearest seat, a tufted satin bench near the stairs.

"Tell us what happened, please, Miss Lowenstein." Joseph jerked his head toward the kitchen, and Mira, nodding, went in search of a stimulant. Jessica looked up at him, putting a hand dazedly to her head. "But you're—we can't have newspapers—"

"I'm a private detective, Miss Lowenstein."

"Oh." She didn't even seem interested, much less surprised.

Mira returned with a good-sized glass of brandy. Jessica drank obediently, and color tinged her pale cheeks for the first time. "He's dead," she said flatly. "But he left a note—everyone's clear."

"Who is dead, Jessica?" breathed Mira. She was leaning forward, her eyes intent on the other's face.

"Ian."

"Ian!" Mira froze.

Jessica sighed and nodded. "After I left here, I went to his place. I told you I thought I knew where the morphine had come from?"

"Go on," said Joseph.

Mira, her cheeks ashen, said nothing.

"I got to thinking I'd overheard Floren say once that through her friends she could get anything she wanted, even drugs, without anyone being the wiser. I accused her of just boasting, and she said: 'Ian can get anything from opium to cocaine through Billy Wong; ask them.' Then she laughed.

"I thought it was just another one of her stories—you know how she was, Mira. But one afternoon I did come into the back hall by the bar and caught Billy hiding something in that broom cupboard. Later on I looked through it but couldn't find anything. Then about a week later old Jorgensen, the janitor," she told Joseph, "came to me and complained someone was deliberately dirtying up his cupboard. I went to see, and there was some powdery stuff spilled in one corner. I smelled it and tasted it, and it was awfully bitter. I thought then it might be dope, but somehow I forgot all about it in the weeks following. We were getting ready for the fashion show—"

"About tonight, Miss Lowenstein—"

She seemed to gather her faculties with an effort, pulling her shoulders erect. "Yes. I went to ask Ian about it. I knew, you see, that he'd done it then. I tried to get in touch with Billy Wong first, but he wasn't home. So I went to see Ian. He didn't answer but the door was unlatched." She moistened her lips; her thin handsome face was lined now and haggard.

"He was in the front room, lying by the bar. There was a note on the bar and a glass—I knew he was dead."

"You didn't touch anything?"

She shook her head.

"And the note?"

"It was typewritten on his stationery. Just, 'I'm to blame for Floren Lawrence and the others. Sorry. Best way out'."

"Was it signed?"

"It had a scrawl at the bottom. I suppose he had written the note before and was reading it over just before he—"

"You have not called the police?"

"No, I came here. I hardly knew what I was doing." She buried her face in her hands.

Joseph left the two women and went to the phone in the den. He called William Reame and, on impulse, phoned Jim Greene as well.

"Meet you there," said Greene shortly. "I think this is it."

"Yes," agreed Joseph.

He went back to the hall.

"I'll borrow your car now, if I may, Miss Hira." She got him the keys. There were tears on her cheeks. Joseph instructed, "Both of you stay here, please. Don't be afraid. Unless I'm very wrong, there's a plainclothesman within call outside, should you need him."

He drove to Renwick's apartment in record time. There was little traffic even on the Strip. Upstairs he found the door still unlatched and saw that the others had not arrived yet.

Rapidly he went through the rooms, stooped over Renwick to feel his heart, his nostrils and sniff briefly at his lips. On top of the bar was one highball glass which he also sniffed. Beneath it, on a sheet of thick deckle-edged stationery with a gilt crest at the top, was the note Jessica had mentioned. The signature in ink was indeed a scrawl; hardly anything could be made of it save the 'I' at the beginning

A square, modern desk in a corner of the living room contained an open portable Royal. The chair was drawn slightly back as if the writer had risen hastily upon completing his work. An open gold fountain pen lay on the blotter.

Joseph went to the medicine chest in the black-tiled bathroom and discovered a prescription box with the label torn off, containing barbiturate tablets. What he wanted was below the washbasin in a built-in storage cabinet, pushed to the back. Two Epsom salt tins containing loose powder. Joseph left them where they were and returned to the living room. He sat down in an armchair and took out Mira Hira's diary, turned to a certain page and began to read a paragraph there.

Reame, followed by his crew, came in just as he put the little book back in his pocket.

"I dunno," growled the inspector, "whether you dream these things up to make me look like a monkey on purpose, or whether they really happen!"

He walked over to Renwick's body and knelt down. Then he waved a hand at his men, got up and, putting a fresh cigar between his brick-red lips, lumbered back to where Joseph sat stolidly upright.

"Well?" There was cold fury in his tone.

"If you don't mind," replied the Indian placidly, "we'll wait for Jim Greene."

"Look, you—this is my territory, get it! I'm in charge. You private eyes think you can skid in and out at will, gumming things up, obstructing justice. Well, I'm goin' to set you straight on a few points!"

"I hope I'm not intruding," said Jim Greene dryly from the door. "The reporters are on their way in force, William, my boy. Better hump to it."

Reame spat out a string of oaths. But he returned to his men to speak briefly and quietly, jabbing orders home with thrusts of his cold cigar.

Jim Greene sighed as he sat down opposite the Indian, and crossed his legs.

Joseph told him briefly about Jessica's hunch and subsequent discovery. He found that the other already knew about Maggie Tally.

"At least this eliminates most of them."

"Yes. Miss Hira was with me. Jessica was with Miss Hira before that. The boy and housekeeper were at the theater. We don't know where the Chinese boy is—or was. But somehow I don't think he fills the bill, even if he was smuggling dope on the side and possibly being blackmailed."

"And Duke Rossi and Bonnie Bartlett are out of it—at least for tonight's work. By the way, the girl is going to be all right. Isn't conscious yet, though."

Two policemen in the doorway began to growl like terriers, linking arms to force a group of men back into the hall.

"Here they are," said Greene, rising. "I'll see what I can do. By the way, isn't that your side-kick, Pierce, out there?"

"Send him in," said Joseph.

"What!"

"I think it may be important."

"It'll start a riot."

"Very well, ask him to meet me downstairs in the lobby—on the quiet."

"Okay, it's your headache." Greene strode to the front door, went outside and closed it firmly behind him. He looked like a gladiator going into battle.

When the tumult outside had subsided to a quiet roar, Joseph eased out the door himself, working his way through reporters clustered avidly about the glib-talking Greene, and plunged down the thickly carpeted staircase.

He found David Pierce pacing up and down the sidewalk, a cigarette stub all but burning his lips.

The reporter spat it onto the curb as he sighted Joseph, and came forward.

"Perhaps we can sit in your car," suggested the Indian. "It will be less conspicuous."

Pierce nodded curtly and led the way down the block to a side street where his battered coupé was parked blatantly too near a fire plug.

When they were seated inside the reporter asked coolly, "Going to give the *Clarion* the scoop?"

"Perhaps. First I'm going to ask a few questions of you and it, and a favor."

"Oh," complained Pierce, "they always do that. Nobody gives you something for nothing Look—we're about ready to go to bed! This could mean my job! Come on, give."

"Suppose you drive me to the *Clarion?* I can talk on the way."

"Okay." Pierce started the motor and ground the gears viciously.

"Did you get the story on Bonnie Bartlett?"

"Sure. I was out there before the rest of those monkeys. Got a tip."

"May I ask who from?"

"I dunno. Some crackpot just phoned the switchboard, and Iron Man Griffith wanted a follow-up, so I went."

Joseph said, "Did you know that Miss Hira's head fitter, Maggie Tally, was murdered tonight around nine o'clock in her home at Venice."

Pierce all but let go of the wheel. "On the level? Jeeze!" He trod heavily on the gas pedal, and the little coupé careened wildly round corners and over car tracks the rest of the way to the *Clarion* building.

Somewhat breathless, Joseph rode up in the slow-moving elevator to the city room. Its beehive activity was in marked contrast to his last visit.

Hector Griffith, in shirt sleeves, a fat cigar rolling between his lips, stood in the open door of his office talking to a middle-aged woman wearing a tweed suit, flat-soled shoes and thick-lensed glasses. There was a black tam on her short-cropped gray hair.

Griffith beckoned imperiously to Pierce and Joseph and stepped back into his office, the woman following.

Pierce gave the editor the gist of his story and Griffith, jumping up from his chair like a wild man, began to shout out orders right and left—into the office phone, out the door to his city editor, to his secretary, to Pierce. Pierce disappeared forthwith.

Joseph sat stolidly in a big leather armchair enjoying this orderly chaos as if he were a visitor from another planet.

In a lull, the woman spoke in her soft, almost whispering voice. "I'll come in later, Mr. Griffith."

"No, wait, Stimms!" roared the editor. "This is going to be something big. May need you. Lots of human interest stuff. Your line in Chicago."

She nodded, her homely face brightening, her blunt, nicotine-stained fingers twining in her tweed lap.

Joseph studied her with interest. Her worn skirt and coat were made of gray tweed, a man's suiting material. She looked as if she had never worn anything else.

"You are from Chicago?" asked Joseph under cover of Hector Griffith's verbal barrage on the telephone. She nodded.

"May I ask if you were a newspaper woman there, too?"

"Yes." It was barely audible.

"Mira Hira and Floren Lawrence also came from Chicago," said Joseph.

Mabel Stimms raised her eyebrows in interrogation.

"Miss Lawrence, it seems, was well known in newspaper circles."

"Oh, yes, she was a celebrity."

"Not only that. Her father was at one time on a newspaper."

Mable looked puzzled, and then a look of wonder took its place. "There was a Jake Lawrence on the *Sun* once, when I was just a cub." She blushed furiously and then labored on in her soft, barely audible voice. "I think he was just a leg man. I don't remember."

"Could he have been on the paper on November 5th, 1937?"

"He could have, I guess. I started on the *Sun* but I was there only a year."

Hector Griffith slammed down the phone, jumped up from his chair and went around to shut the office door and lock it. The confusion and clatter outside dimmed to a steady but bearable hum. Hector returned to his chair, rubbing his hands.

"Now, let's have what you've got, Joe. You listen in, Stimms; maybe you'll get a hunch where to start."

Joseph related the night's happenings.

"I think I'll start with Mira Hira and Jessica Lowenstein," murmured Mabel Stimms.

"Good idea. Make it good—and for Pete's sake spare the adjectives and put in a few bare facts."

Mabel grinned. She got up and shut the door softly behind her.

"Good gal," said Griffith. "Now, anything to spill on the side, Joe?"

"Yes. Have you any recollection of a Jake Lawrence once employed by the *Chicago Sun?*"

Griffith screwed up his face. "No, can't say I have. Why?"

"Let me ask the questions first. Have you got anybody on the staff who was employed by the *Sun* during the '30s?"

"Don't think so. But I'll check. Why?"

Joseph, ignoring the question, asked, "Can you get me a copy of the *Sun* for November 5th, 1937?"

Griffith's eyes narrowed. "Maybe. It'll take time. But why in—?"

"We haven't got much time. Get at it, will you, please?"

The editor turned to his phone and began to speak swiftly and clearly into it. When Joseph rose and went to the door, he barked, "Hey! Where you goin'? I may need you—"

"Phone me at City Hall. I'll be in Greene's office." Joseph went out and closed the door on Griffith's grumbling epithets.

He was stepping into the elevator a moment later when a lean arm jerked him by the elbow. Pierce, in shirt-sleeves, panting, and with his coat dangling from one hand, said: "Hey! Where to?"

"I'm on my way to Headquarters," Joseph told him.

"I'll drive you, pal. I'm not losing you tonight!"

"You can drive me down, but I think you'll be out of luck getting in on the conference."

"Okay. I'll wait outside like a good little boy."

On the way down Joseph turned to the reporter. "Ian Renwick was a friend of yours, wasn't he?"

"Was he?" asked Pierce, staring fixedly at the floor.

Joseph noted that his hands shook in spite of a mighty effort to control them, and his nostrils looked pinched and white. The reporter began suddenly to roll down his shirt sleeves, jamming his arms into his coat.

"Here we are," he growled.

CHAPTER XV

A uniformed policeman entered and told Greene, "There's a couple outside, sir—" he consulted a notebook—"Yates-Wolfton. Want to see you, sir."

"Show them in," said Greene at once.

Joseph sat up straighter in his chair. Reame looked puzzled as he got out a fresh cigar. Jim Greene called, "Come in," when the young cop knocked again.

Mrs. Yates-Wolfton swept into the room like a dreadnaught trailing a tug. She eyed the best chair, from which Reame rose automatically, and settled herself majestically, drawing a vast chinchilla cape about her mountainous shoulders. She wore a white satin evening gown beneath the cape, white satin slippers, and a blinding array of diamonds.

The thin, white-haired, wavering old man who followed her was faultlessly attired in evening clothes, like a dummy dressed for a window display. A monocle was screwed into one watery blue eye. He sank into the chair Joseph offered with a sigh of senile satisfaction.

Mrs. Yates-Wolfton swung her large head and shrewd eyes between the three men facing her. "We were at the opera tonight. Afterwards we dropped into a friend's for supper. We heard what has been happening concerning certain friends of ours. This scandal about Mira Hira must stop! The girl is innocent."

"M'dear!" mumbled Lord Gordon.

"I must speak, Gordon."

The old man sighed quaveringly and fingered his lower lip.

"Have you anything to tell us?" prompted Jim Greene.

"I most certainly have, young man! As you know, I was one of the last persons to leave Mira's the night Floren Lawrence died. I was on the second floor in a fitting room."

"You saw something?" asked Reame, leaning forward expectantly.

"Certainly not! I was alone on the second floor, dressing. I was in a hurry to meet dear Gordon at the Ambassador for cocktails. We were dining at Howard Mantley's at nine."

"At Mantley's?" echoed Greene with interest.

"Yes. He's a very old friend."

"Yet you were not there," said Joseph, "the night of his last big party—the night Edgar Vorman was killed?"

Mrs. Yates-Wolfton put up a large white gloved hand. "Of course not. We were aboard our yacht, the *Yolanda*. We started on a week's cruise, but poor Gordon's stomach couldn't stand it, so we put back to Newport at once." She threw her husband a smile.

"I see."

"No, I fear you don't. As dear Gordon has so often remarked, the police are prone to blunder from one foolish mistake to the other."

Lord Gordon spluttered ineffectually behind a blue-veined hand, but his forthright wife went boldly on.

"People in office are often so addle-pated. You can't say that Mira Hira had anything to do with these ghastly murders. I can prove it!"

"Is that so?" asked Reame crossly.

"Certainly, Constable. Do you doubt my veracity?"

"My dear," said his lordship unhappily.

"Gordon, darling, please leave this to me. This is my country, after all."

"May I ask what proof you have of Miss Hira's innocence?" asked Greene sharply.

"I didn't see anything while I was in the shop that night."

The three men relaxed visibly.

"But I heard something. The lift—the elevator—going up to the tower."

"Do you know the time?" questioned Joseph.

"Certainly. I have a most accurate watch, made for me by the Royal Jeweler. It was exactly a quarter of seven."

The three detectives exchanged swift glances.

"Furthermore," added the big woman, "the lift did not come down again while I was there, a matter of five minutes. I walked to the main floor—good for my liver—and I knocked at Mira's door to say good-night. When I got no response I went in. The poor child was stretched out on her couch sound asleep."

"She could've been shamming," growled Reame.

"My dear man, no one can pretend in front of me and get away with it. My poor father used to try that ruse, but it never worked—the eyelids, y'know. It would take a Yogi to control them completely, and even then—"

"I don't believe it," snapped Reame. "Maybe she didn't actually do the murders, but she was in on the deal somewhere. Her place was a natural for peddling dope."

"My dear man, can you possibly be serious? Do you imagine that I patronize dope dens?"

"You might not've known, lady."

Mrs. Yates-Wolfton's glance was as potent as an acetylene torch. Even Reame was suitably withered by it. His eyes dropped, while his face took on the color of a cooked beet. Making an excuse, he departed on some mission of his own.

"Now," said the lady, twisting her chinchillaed shoulders, "am I to understand that poor Mira is cleared of these ridiculous charges? I would have come to you sooner, but we were completely out of touch aboard the *Yolanda*."

Green spoke soothingly. "For some time now most of us have been inclined to exclude Mira Hira as a suspect."

"Ah! Then Gordon and I can retire in peace." She rose like Atlantis coming up from the sea, the foam of her white skirt twirling about monumental ankles. "Come, Gordon!"

"Eh? Wot, m'dear?" His lordship awoke with a guilty start, searching the room foggily for his wife's familiar bulk. Having located it, he rose with a slightly trembling motion and followed his wife from the room.

The phone shrilled on the desk. Greene took it up, then passed the instrument to Joseph.

"Yes?"

"Joe? Hector Griffith. No record of any ex-Chicago employees. Mostly local Coast talent—few New Yorkers. Haven't located that copy of the *Chi Sun* for you yet."

"Keep trying," urged Joseph, and rang off.

"Well?"

"It was Griffith at the *Clarion*. He's trying to find out a few things for me."

"Such as—"

But Joseph was suddenly diverted. He reached across and picked up the keyring. "No one carries an empty keyring." The coin was worn and old-looking, the size of a fifty-cent piece. The carvings swelled its sides. Joseph manipulated it gently between lean bronzed fingers. Then he sat very still, feeling it move on either side, not once but twice, three times. Carefully he brought the two halves apart. A folded piece of paper spilled onto Greene's carpet. With an oath the latter stooped to pick it up. He unfolded it and spread it on his desk, while he and Joseph read the contents, and then were suddenly galvanized into activity. Joseph raced out of the office, while Greene, sombre-eyed and quick-lipped, issued surprising orders over the phone.

A few seconds later, Greene found Joseph in the outer office using the phone there.

"I've sent a cab," he heard him say. "Get up there as soon as you can." He hung up and dialed another number. "Griffith—tell him it's Joe. Hello, Hector—how long has Stimms worked for you? She came directly from Chicago, didn't she? Thanks." He looked grim when he slammed down the phone. "Let's get going."

"You bet," said Greene.

Downstairs in the wide foyer, they found David Pierce patiently waiting. Joseph, eyeing the reporter narrowly, said: "If you still want that exclusive, you'd better come along with us."

The police car moved down Sunset at top speed. No siren was necessary at this hour, a few minutes after three, when the wide street appeared oddly deserted.

They turned up Mira's driveway through a mist that had just gathered. Long dripping branches of pepper and toyon and eucalyptus flicked ghostly fingertips across the car's hard top. Up above some-where a mourning dove called plaintively.

A battered Ford was drawn up in the drive, but the front of the big house, at least, was in total darkness.

Joseph was the first out. He raced on light feet to the door and put his finger on the bell, keeping it there.

The door was opened presently by Francine Webb, wearing a housecoat and slippers. She looked startled. "Yes?"

"We must see Miss Hira at once."

"At this hour! My goodness, what on earth—" Without waiting, Joseph crowded in the door, followed by Greene and Pierce.

Francine bristled. "You reporters ought to be horsewhipped! Dis-turbing decent citizens like this! Really, I thought after being cordial to one of you—"

"I'm not a reporter, Miss Webb. And this is Inspector Greene, of the Los Angeles police."

"Well, even so, I don't see—"

"We must speak to Miss Hira at once," said Greene, closing the door firmly behind him. "Please call her."

"I'm afraid that won't be possible."

"Why not?"

"She is asleep."

"Wake her." It was an order.

Francine shook her head. "I'm afraid you don't understand. She's taken a sedative."

Joseph pushed by the housekeeper and bounded up the stairs two at a time. In the upper hall Sean fell into his arms, rigid with fear.

"Joe!" he panted. "Joe!"

"Sean, what is it?"

"Mom," the boy sobbed. "My Mom's killed herself!" His voice choked on the words and went tumbling on. "I couldn't sleep. S-some-one's been downstairs talkin' to Fran. I came out to see who it was, but I couldn't hear from the stairs, so I went into M-Mom's room. She left a note on her desk. She isn't even breathing!"

"Sean," said the Indian firmly, "I'm going to ask you to be brave and help me for a little while. Go into your room and stay there until

I send for you. I won't be long. It's a great deal to ask, but I know you can do it."

The boy wiped his face on the sleeve of his robe, nodded and turned stiffly away. Joseph waited until he had disappeared inside his own room and he heard the latch click. Then he turned swiftly into Mira's room.

She lay like a child, half on her side, her long dark hair in two braids. She was cold to the touch, her pupils dilated. Joseph turned her over and began artificial respiration. If there was a chance. . . .

Greene, bounding into the room a moment later, took in the situation at a glance. Joseph motioned to him with his head and Greene took over as the Indian's strong dark hands relinquished their hold. He was panting slightly, beads of moisture beading his brow and upper lip.

"Is she—" began Greene jerkily.

"Yes. Keep it up!" Joseph bent to sniff a glass on the bedside table. Morphine.

He went to the desk and took up the phone. His terse call for a police ambulance and doctor completed, he lifted the single sheet of typewriter paper between his fingernails, and read the typed words carefully.

> Sorry things have to end like this, but I can't go on. My
> life was over when Ian died. Fran dear, try to under-
> stand, and look after Sean. You are to be his guardian.
> Love to you both—

The message was roughly initialed M.H.

Joseph returned to the bed. Mira, a faint pearl-like glow in her cheeks, was breathing faintly, a labored unsteady breath, but Joseph felt like shouting with delight.

"Hope doctor won't be long!" panted Greene.

"I'll spell you in a minute. She's making it all right. I've got to do a couple of things. Can you carry on?"

"Sure. Go ahead. Say—reporter, Stimms, downstairs—been here hour."

Joseph nodded grimly, then turned toward Mira's bathroom. There was no trace of morphine in the medicine cabinet. He remembered the diary, and delved beneath towels once more to the bottom of the cupboard. He brought up an Epsom salt tin. Using as much care as possible, he opened it, touched a speck of the powder to his tongue and hastily spat in the sink. Taking the tin with him, he went out through the bedroom again, noting with satisfaction that Mira's breathing was stronger. He walked down the hall to Francine's room and went inside. Next door he could hear Sean's muffled sobs, and the Indian's jaws tightened.

Swiftly but thoroughly he went through the gay little room, finally taking with him the typewriter from the closet, and two other items.

The front doorbell was ringing when he paused at Sean's room to tell him his mother was going to be all right.

"Honest, Joe?" Sean stared through swollen eyelids, but the rigid fear seemed to drain out of him as he stood there.

"Honest Injun, Sean. Now be a good fellow and stay here for a little while longer."

The boy nodded and moved back into his room as Joseph started down the stairs. He passed the doctor and two stretcher bearers on his way. Below, staring up like wondering children, were Francine, Mabel Stimms and David Pierce.

"Why," began Francine, "what in the world are you doing with my—"

"Please go and call the maid, Miss Webb."

"I'll do no such thing! I'm going upstairs this instant to Mira! That doctor said she's very ill. I can't imagine—"

Joseph spoke crisply. "You will follow instructions, Miss Webb. Police instructions."

At his tone the housekeeper fell back a pace. "I don't like this," she murmured. "What's wrong? What's happened to Mira? Whatever it is, you must let me go up to Sean. He's there all alone."

"I've seen to the boy. Now please call the maid."

Francine moved off uncertainly.

"What is it?" whispered Mabel Stimms, a wary strained expression on her face.

"Later," said Joseph. "I want you two to go into the den and wait."

The reporters exchanged eloquent glances, but they proved more cooperative than the housekeeper. When she returned a moment later with Emerald, dressed in a cerise satin robe, Joseph ushered them both into the den and shut the door on Francine's remonstrances.

The doctor came down the stairs with his patient blanket-wrapped on the stretcher. "Think she'll do," he growled as he passed.

Joseph and Greene stood in the doorway while the big ambulance turned and whisked off down the drive, its red eyes winking through the mist.

"That was close," sighed Greene, wiping his face with a handkerchief. "Now look, Joe, this whole thing may hang together for you, but I'm frank in saying as far as I'm concerned, there are a heck of a lot of left over pieces!"

"I'll explain, Jim, but let me do it my own way. I want you to phone Reame and tell him to get up here fast. It's important."

"Okay," sighed Greene. "If you say so—but I think it's crazy." He turned toward the den, but Joseph stopped him. "Use the kitchen phone."

A moment later the front doorbell rang. Joseph answered it promptly, noting the taxi at the foot of the steps.

"I came as soon as I could," said the woman.

"Thank you." Joseph put a bill in the driver's hand and led the woman inside. "I want you to look at something," he said, "and tell me if you have ever seen it before."

Almarina Bagley moistened her lips and stared down at the object he held out in his palm.

"Why, yeah, sure. That's Floren Lawrence's! Mr. Renwick had it made for her once from an old coin or something. It unscrews. She useta keep things in it."

"Things?"

"Well," the woman's eyes skittered from right to left, "aspirins sometimes, stamps—anything she was afraid she'd lose in her purse." She was breathing heavily and not quite steadily. "Can I go now? I don't see what all this is to you anyway. I wouldn'ta come, only you said—"

"I'm afraid I used a ruse to get you here. I'm a detective. This has to do with murder. Will you please wait in that room over there? And refrain from mentioning this little matter?"

Almarina, her jaw slack, moved away like a sleepwalker.

When Jim Greene came into the hall again he found Joseph pecking away at a portable typewriter. "What gives?"

"Another piece of the puzzle," grinned the Indian. "I've got two phone calls to make; then I'm through. Wait here for Reame. When he comes, take him into the den there, and take these things along with you. Be careful of the can; it's morphine."

"What!"

"No questions now, Jim," pleaded the other.

"Okay, I'll wait."

Joseph touched him on the shoulder and went off toward the kitchen. The big room sparkled clinically in the overhead lights.

One call went through without a hitch and got him his answer in minutes. The other took a good deal longer, several calls in fact, and netted him only dubious satisfaction. But it was enough. He straightened his shoulders and took a deep breath as he walked out of the room.

The babble of voices inside the den ceased as the Indian stepped inside and closed the door.

Reame crouched on the edge of a leather chair by the door. Greene sat opposite him smoking a cigarette. Francine and Mabel Stimms sat side by side in the window seat. Almarina Bagley and Emerald occupied straight chairs near the bookcase. David Pierce lounged against the wall nearby.

Joseph went to the desk where Greene had deposited the items he had requested him to bring in.

He spoke quietly. "I'm not going to give you a lecture, or make a speech. But for those of you who don't know, Mira Hira was poisoned tonight with morphine."

"No!" whispered Mabel Stimms. "But I've been here—"

David Pierce stood tautly against the wall, his face pale.

Francine rose unsteadily. "And you wouldn't let me go to her! How heartless—how despicable!" She sank back to her seat.

"She's in good hands," said Joseph gently.

Francine buried her face in her hands.

Almarina Bagley said crossly, "What's all this got to do with me?"

"Did she leave a note?" asked Mabel Stimms.

"Yes. There was a note."

Pierce roused himself, looking suddenly hollow-eyed. "She tried to kill herself because of Renwick—that it?"

"She did not try to kill herself. I said there was a note, and that Miss Hira suffered from morphine poisoning. There was even a can of morphine, this one, hidden in her bedroom."

"Then—"

"It was very clever planning on the part of someone who tried to kill her. It almost worked. But there was bad timing—a characteristic of this criminal."

"What do you mean?" asked Reame, biting off the words.

"I mean," said Joseph, "that in spite of a very logical mind, this person is highly impulsive."

Reame sat back in his chair, an odd expression on his brick-colored face.

Joseph went on:

"Let's start with Floren Lawrence's death, a hard one to crack, because someone could have slipped morphine into her drink some little time before she actually took it. Ian Renwick, for one, had mixed a special concoction he called Andale, and Floren's was still there untouched when he, Vorman and Rossi left her. Any of them might have put the narcotic into her drink. But Vorman himself was killed soon after, and Floren's death aided neither Renwick nor Rossi. Rossi seemed genuinely fond of her and even hired me to trace her death.

"As to why she was killed, we could only guess that she was blackmailing someone, or was so dangerous to someone for some other reason that she had to be silenced at once.

"I knew that in spite of the circumstances, this was not a planned murder. It had all the marks of an impulsive, daring, spur-of-the-moment crime. Since the men were eliminated in my mind, I concentrated on the employees. Only Jessica Lowenstein and Maggie Tally, plus Mira, were present that night. I could discover no motive for the two employees. There was a single woman customer on the second floor, but she seemed innocent enough. I decided that some other employee might have returned to the shop later, but it seemed unlikely. The risk was too great.

"Mira Hira had, of course, opportunity. For a time she and Floren Lawrence were alone on the premises. They were not fond of each other, and Floren had hinted that she had something to reveal to her. But we have the word of Mrs. Yates-Wolfton that Mira was asleep in her office at ten minutes of seven. The elevator, obviously carrying the murderer, had gone upstairs five minutes before and had not come down."

"This is all hearsay, Joe, not proof," Greene reminded him.

"I'm trying to paint the picture around the proof."

Reame moved restlessly but said nothing. He seemed thoughtful and uneasy.

"The murderer had to have access to the shop, be familiar with it, and know that Floren Lawrence was alone in the tower asleep. That still left a wide field, but little things began to point in a certain direction," said Joseph. "Edgar Vorman, highly excited, phoned Mira and made a secret appointment with her at Howard Mantley's tea house on the night of the latter's party. The killer, suspecting rightly that Vorman held vital information which he meant to pass on to Mira, panicked and, following Vorman, committed yet another abortive murder."

"But if it was someone at Howard Mantley's, how did they get in? It was by invitation only—unless you mean a guest," asked David Pierce slowly.

"Yes. But as at all such large affairs, it was practically impossible to watch all entrances and exits. The front door, it was true, was manned by the Negro butler. But *you* succeeded in entering without an invitation, didn't you, Mr. Pierce?"

Pierce flushed and looked away. "But I was—"

"Then there was the back door and service entrance, not too difficult to manage. A great many extra servants are hired for a party like that. I've just phoned Mr. Mantley and found that there were at least twenty persons hired for the night, all complete strangers to the household staff."

A movement went through his little audience.

"Again, Mira Hira could have been a perfect suspect. She had opportunity surely, and perhaps motive. But I later discovered that Ian Renwick had a like chance and an even stronger motive. And the murderer—again on a frightened impulse—made the fatal mistake of attempting to kill Miss Hira soon after that, on the Palos Verdes highway. This, as far as the police were concerned, virtually cleared her of being a murderess."

Greene gently put down his cigar and leaned forward. His eye swept the rigid, listening faces in the little group and came back to Joseph's dark taciturn visage.

"And another danger threatened—real live evidence this time. Maggie Tally discovered it quite by accident the night of Floren's death. Maggie communicated with Mira, and again the murderer, realizing what the evidence was, leaped impulsively. Maggie was killed by someone she knew, but the killer missed finding the evidence in the short amount of time allowed for the crime. I was more fortunate."

Again that little stir of muscles flexing.

"Now it was really necessary for a sop to the police. So the death of Ian Renwick was rigged. He was killed for that reason, and because he had become a danger to the murderer.

"But in many ways his death backfired. The police were closing in. And then a piece of stupendous luck came along. Bonnie Bartlett was found in Floren Lawrence's apartment, with a fractured skull, and all evidence pointing to Duke Rossi as the attacker. It looked as if Bonnie, alerted by her maid, Almarina, and knowing Floren's habits, had come to the apartment to get Floren's clippings. In the eyes of the law it appeared that the murderer could not allow her to complete her search.

"I found the clippings later, however, and there was nothing about Mr. Rossi at all. His clothes were searched at headquarters and yielded nothing He could, of course, have hidden the evidence away in the apartment while we sat there, but a minute search later disproved that possibility.

"There was, however, a clipping about you, Almarina."

The woman had gone very white. Her mouth opened and closed like a fish out of water.

"I didn't—"

"There was a clipping of the '20s mentioning several thefts at the Roxy Theater in New York. A dresser was under suspicion. You were afraid, weren't you, Almarina, that Bonnie would discover it? Floren had held it over you for years, I suppose."

Almarina began to cry.

"You may as well tell us," Joseph said softly. "It will be better in the end."

"Yes. She knew. I was dresser for another actress then—a headliner. Floren was a movie star making a guest appearance. She found out about me. She said she was probably the only one who knew positively, and she wouldn't talk if I'd work for her. I did—for years, at no salary." Almarina's hands closed convulsively on her worn black bag. "I hated her, but I didn't kill her. She let me go finally, turned me out when I was old and penniless, because she was getting up in the world and didn't like me around reminding her of old times. I went to Bonnie Bartlett; she was good to me."

"You had kept a key to the apartment, just as Bonnie had?"

Almarina nodded dumbly.

"When you heard Bonnie was going there to hunt through Floren's things and see what she could find, you were afraid she would see the theft clipping. You wanted to keep your job, and you intended merely to stun Bonnie, destroy the clipping and leave?"

"So help me, I wouldn't'ta hurt her that bad—"

"You didn't realize the deadly weight of the bronze paperweight you used."

"Oh God!"

"Before you could start your search for the clips, Duke Rossi grew impatient and came in. We weren't far behind him. You were trapped—in one of the bedrooms, I think."

"Under the guest bed," moaned Almarina.

Joseph nodded. "You slipped out when the police left. I was still there but you didn't know it. I heard a faint noise. I should have investigated."

Reame said, "Is all this on the level?"

Almarina nodded miserably.

"Then who's the murderer?" demanded Mabel Stimms.

"I was quite interested in you, Miss Stimms, when we first met. You were on the scene the day Floren died, and the night Vorman was killed as well, weren't you?"

Mabel flushed to the roots of her grey hair.

"I thought when we met I recognized you as having been a guest at Mantley's. Did she get in with you, Pierce?"

"Well—"

"You both crashed, shall we say, on the strength of Ian Renwick's invitation?"

"What if we did?" snapped David Pierce. "Renwick was a friend of mine—newspaper people have to use what methods they can. They're seldom 'invited' to cover a story!"

"Right. But Renwick was more than a friend of yours, Mr. Pierce; he was by way of being your master."

"What the devil do you mean?"

"Will you roll up your sleeves, Mr. Pierce?"

"No, why should I?" The reporter's lips were trembling. "What is this!"

"Tonight as we left the *Clarion* you were indiscreet enough to come after me in your shirtsleeves with the sleeves rolled up. I saw the unmistakable puncture marks of the hypodermic on your arms—both of them—a good many. You are a dope addict, are you not? And Renwick was your supplier. He found cause to use you because of this; you were a valuable informant."

Pierce stiffened and then lowered his eyes. "I'm sunk anyway—what difference does it make? Sure he used me."

"Why, you lousy liar," stormed Reame. "Tryin' to hoodwink me with your 'deals' and exclusives! I oughta ram my fist down your throat." The sheriff's man half-rose, but Greene shoved him back in his seat.

"Floren once boasted," went on the Indian, "that she could obtain dope easily, and Jessica Lowenstein found narcotics at Mira Hira's. She suspected the Chinese boy, Billy Wong, but he was only a cog in Ian Renwick's wheel. He had been peddling narcotics for years. In Chicago to begin with, and then here when he and Mira moved West. He had a perfect front for it, the highest connections and no breath of suspicion attached to him.

"But to get back to you, Miss Stimms. You were also from Chicago, and a fine newspaper woman. Yet you left a good job doing straight reporting to come out here and take over the comparatively inconsequential one of fashion reporter on the Clarion. I wondered why."

"My health," flushed Mabel Stimms.

"Yet you appear perfectly healthy?"

"I'm not! I have heart trouble—"

"Yet none of the earmarks of that disease. No, I believe you came here to try a spot of blackmail, yourself."

"You're lying!" Mabel's voice rose to a raw screech. "I didn't—I didn't!"

"Did you come here tonight to continue your blackmailing or, failing that, to kill Miss Hira?"

"I didn't! She was asleep when I got here! I never saw her tonight."

"Did you ask to see her?"

"Yes," said Francine, "but I couldn't let her. Poor Mira had retired, completely worn out, hours before. I didn't want to be rude to Miss Stimms, so I showed her in here and we talked for a while."

"I see. Did you leave Miss Stimms at any time?"

"No—yes, for only a moment. I thought I heard Emerald prowling around in the hall. I went out to see."

"I don't do no prowlin'," sulked Emerald. "You always listenin' at folks—"

"Emerald, I will not have this conduct," said Francine primly. Then she faced Greene. "I know you are from the police—you and this other gentleman." She nodded toward Reame. "But may I ask what right *this* man has to assume authority?"

"He is a private detective who is helping us," said Greene dryly. Out of the corner of his eye he could see Reame's face growing red. Serves him right, he thought grimly.

"Oh," said Francine. "Well, he does seem to ramble on and prove nothing. And poor little Sean upstairs all alone. Really, I must go to him." She rose and started across the room. "You might," she told Joseph haughtily, "stop wasting your time and everyone else's and find this wretched murderer."

As she passed, Joseph held out his palm; in it rested the coin key-ring. "Did you ever see this before, Miss Webb?"

She glanced at it briefly. "No, why should I have?"

"Because I think you would find it highly interesting."

"Oh?"

With a deft twist of his fingers he undid the little double talisman and took out the folded piece of paper.

Francine, standing like a statue, her round blue eyes distended, suddenly reached out to tear the clipping from his fingers and ripped it to shreds.

"Yes," said Joseph softly, when Reame had come forward with a mighty oath and seized the woman's arms. "This was what you were afraid Floren was going to show to Mira. It could have upset all your plans, couldn't it? She had to die because she had stumbled onto your secret. Was Floren ever alone in your room?"

"Yes," panted the woman.

"And she was a natural ferret? She heartlessly searched your things and found something? But she didn't remove the evidence. She knew where she could get some of her own, just as good. And then she could use it whenever she chose.

"When Mira phoned you about having to stay on at the shop to fit Floren, she also told you the actress had hinted at something special she wanted to tell her. You made your plans accordingly, swiftly—and I will add, with great daring. You took incredible chances that first time, but the speed and accuracy with which you acted saved you and threw the authorities off the scent."

Francine stirred but she seemed not to be listening.

"At approximately 6:20 you spoke to Mira on the phone. You went directly to the shop, knowing that except for Mira, only Jessica and Maggie would be there. You have copies of all Mira's keys—an easy thing to manage when you occupy the same house as a privileged guest. I found keys in your dresser to Renwick's apartment and to Floren's, too. You were most thorough, Miss Webb.

"You went in the back entrance and took the morphine from the place you knew Ian and Billy Wong usually secreted it, and one of the silver cups from Ian's cocktail set. Then you went up in the elevator, at a quarter to seven. Mrs. Yates-Wolfton heard you. She was on the second floor, dressing.

"You used your pass-key to get into the tower, not noticing till later that you had ripped your tweed coat on the elevator door and dropped a shred of material on the hall floor. Inside, you must have tried to argue with Floren in a friendly fashion while you slipped the narcotic unseen into the drink Ian left. You offered to drink a parting toast with the bemused Floren. She agreed, no doubt, and once she had drunk the poison and collapsed, you made a swift and fruitless search of her person and things. Fruitless because Edgar Vorman, who knew Floren and her ways, had recognized the coin in her purse earlier, and being suspicious of her actions anyway, had carried it off with him. You pressed Floren's fingers to and put down the innocent cup you had brought up with you and carried away the one Floren had used. Even so, you had been longer than you wanted to be. It was nearly seven, and Mira had said she would waken Floren at seven. It must have been nearly that when you left the shop.

"It was only a few minutes past when you entered the library and exchanged a book. The librarian remembers you—if you could have counted on that you need not have engineered that little parking accident around 7:30 outside the library door.

"You took your time getting back to the shop, but even so, they had only just discovered the crime, due to Mira's having overslept."

"How about Vorman and that Maggie dame?" Reame wanted to know.

"Vorman very foolishly phoned Mira from this very room to make his appointment. Miss Webb was listening and naturally surmised he had taken the clipping from Floren or found it somewhere. She couldn't take a chance. She got into Mantley's by the service entrance. She knew Mantley's house because she had been there with Mira. She slipped outside and waited near the path to the tea house. Ian Renwick must have caused her a moment's panic when he sauntered down and joined Mira. He left in time, however, and when Vorman finally came along she was ready for him.

"There was nothing that looked like clippings on him—she didn't know about Floren's freak keyring—and again she had to abandon the search. She may have thought she was safe by then. She left the garden and was at home awaiting Mira when the latter got here.

"She had grown suspicious of everyone, though, and when Mira became rather secretive and said offhandedly that she was going for a drive and didn't know when she'd get back, Miss Webb followed her, having tampered with a few wires and drained out half the gas in Mira's car the night before upon her return from Mantley's, just in case Mira should have to be stopped.

"When the car stalled, and Miss Webb saw her opportunity—a purely spur of the moment action, by the way—she tried to run her down. She undoubtedly thought that she had killed her."

Joseph picked up a tweed coat from the desk and brought the scrap of tweed Maggie had found from his pocket.

"These match, Miss Webb, just as you feared they might. You discovered that you had ripped your coat on the night Floren was killed, didn't you? Here is where you mended it, but it is slightly puckered. When Mira told you, or you heard, that Maggie had found something in the hall of the tower, you guessed what it was.

"Again you panicked, and once more your sheer daring helped you out—temporarily. You took Sean to the theater the night Maggie was killed. I have no doubt that the boy will tell us the theater was in Venice, and that at some time during the performance, you excused yourself to go to the ladies' room. Even if Sean grew restive or curious and came out, he couldn't follow you into the ladies' room. And if he should happen to see you coming in the front door again, you could complain of a headache and say you had been out for air. It was a sound, if not a perfect alibi. Daring carried it through. A boy intent on a motion picture couldn't swear how long you had been gone.

"But like all killers, your fears and suspicions grew with each crime you committed. You knew that Ian Renwick was a danger to you, and that he was growing more unreliable. There was a chance he might break down and tell Mira everything. So you went to have a talk with him. And in your quiet, disarming way you managed to put a death-dealing narcotic into his drink. You then typed out the supposed suicide note on his machine, wearing your gloves all this time without doubt—there were none of your fingerprints in the apartment. Then you scrawled his signature on the bottom of the page.

You knew that there were narcotics on the premises, which would strengthen suspicion against Renwick.

"David Pierce, when he joined me downstairs the night Renwick died, was suspicious and afraid. He attached himself to me on the spot, and quite by accident later in the night I discovered his secret. Dope.

"Even though luck had played into your hands, and police suspicion had settled on Duke Rossi, you, Miss Webb, decided to end the game once and for all, to ensure your safety and your fortune. You expected to be alone here tonight. You drugged Mira in the manner you had intended for—shall we say, eleven years? It was so simple to do. You were her best friend, a trusted member of her family."

Francine shuddered but her eyes, wide and staring, were held by the Indian's inscrutable black ones, like a bird held in hypnotic trance by a snake.

"Even so, you made one more mistake, Miss Webb," continued Joseph softly. "In writing her 'suicide' note, Mira would surely have used her own machine. She had an up-to-date portable in her own closet. I saw it some days ago when I first searched her rooms. Typewriters leave their own unmistakable trail, Miss Webb, a damning one in this case. Tonight I typed out a line on your machine; even a casual observer can see that type matches that of the suicide note. I also found this small silver cup in the top of your closet—one of the set Ian Renwick kept at Mira's shop. I have no doubt it will still show traces of the poison."

"But why?" asked David Pierce wonderingly, "Why did she do it all?"

"For money—and revenge," answered Joseph simply.

"What was in that damned clipping?" growled Reame. He looked ready to burst.

"The 1937 notice of a divorce between Francine Webb Renwick and Ian Renwick. She made the mistake of keeping her marriage license in her bedroom. That was what Floren Lawrence discovered and decided to check on through her newspaper friends. When she got the information she wanted she put it aside to use at her discretion. She didn't want it for blackmail, but to smash Mira's marriage completely and destroy her faith in her cherished housekeeper-friend. Miss Webb, when she guessed what was afoot, probably from remarks Ian made, realized that Mira would never forgive her duplicity, and her chances or remaining safely in Mira's will, a long-time plan of hers, depended upon her stopping Miss Lawrence. No wonder she went to such lengths to act at once, the moment Mira phoned that night and told her about Floren.

"She was married to Renwick in 1936, for the space of a few months; then he deserted her. But she meant to get even and she meant to have him back. It was a double blow when he married her friend and roommate, Mira Hira, and showed himself genuinely in love. She determined to get even with them both.

"In the brief span of her own marriage to Renwick, she had discovered that he was passing dope, and after he married Mira, Miss Webb must have confronted him with the fact and held it as a lever against him ever after."

Francine threw back her head suddenly and began to speak in a strange harsh voice.

"He was a liar and a cheat! He never had any income from abroad; they'd chucked him out years before. All his income came from dope!" She laughed gratingly. "But he was afraid he'd lose his precious Mira, so he played along with me. He told me if I'd be patient and wait until Mira's shop made enough money, he'd get a divorce and marry me. He'd get half her property under California law. He was a liar. He never meant to do it, I found out! But I had a better plan. I saw his marriage broken up all right, and Mira was sore enough to change her will. I saw to it he didn't get anything—I'd have gotten it all! There was money for me in the will all right, but the rest, all of it, went to Sean. With Ian and Mira dead, I'd have had the boy—as his guardian. It's in her will!"

In a lower tone she added, "I hated her—I always hated her! She took everything that should have been mine. This house—it was really *my* house. *I* ran it. *I* took care of it. *I* loved it! All she cared about was her precious shop. Even the boy—I was more mother to him than *she* ever was!"

She jerked erect suddenly in Reame's grasp, then sank to her knees, her eyes rolling, flecks of saliva on her lips.

While Reame and David Pierce carried her from the room, her head lolling strangely like a broken doll's, Joseph turned to face Mabel Stimms.

"You knew Francine Webb in Chicago, didn't you?"

"I—yes." It was barely a whisper.

"You stumbled on the fact that she had been married to Ian Renwick, now the wife of a famous designer. You came out here on speculation, and discovered your old friend was not only here, but was acting as housekeeper to the second Mrs. Renwick.

"You glanced back through the records, and found that when Ian and Mira were married there was no mention of a previous marriage for either. This setup looked, and was, perfect for blackmail. Isn't this true, Miss Stimms?"

All the fight went out of her; she seemed to sag in her rumpled tweed suit, like a scarecrow with the stuffing leaking out. She sat for a moment staring stonily at her blunt, nicotine-stained fingers; then she said flatly, "It's—yes, it's true."

Greene crossed the room and put an arm across the Indian's broad shoulders. "Joe, what a nest of rattlesnakes you've stirred up for us. I think Willie Reame's as flabbergasted as I am! Do you just dream these things up, or do they come to you in the witching hour?"

"I just stick to the trail," smiled Joseph.

CHAPTER XVI

At the door, the nurse paused and said quietly, "The doctor says you may see her; she's out of danger. She really was very lucky. Someone caught her just in the nick of time."

Joseph followed a wide-eyed Sean into the dimly lighted white room. Mira smiled wanly back at them from a high white bed. There were dark smudges under her eyes, and her skin still had a peculiar pearly glow, but over Sean's head as it nestled against her breast, she spoke to Joseph in stronger tones than he had expected.

He took the chair by the bed and told her briefly what had happened.

"Fran!" she breathed. "Fran? It's all so dreadfully clear now, isn't it? Will they release him now—Mr. Rossi?" It was a shy, almost self-conscious question.

"Yes."

"I'm glad." After a time she said, "What about Fran?"

"She will stand trial, if she doesn't go to an asylum. I don't say that she's crazy, but she is obviously unbalanced. She suffered some sort of fit or stroke tonight."

"How awful."

The door behind Joseph opened and he saw Mira's expressive face register warm delight. A film of rosy color washed over the pale cheeks.

"Duke!"

"Mira! I came as soon as I—"

Sean raised his head. His mother said, "Duke, this is my son, Sean. Darling, a friend of Mother's, Mr. Rossi."

"Hi, Sean."

"Mr. Rossi lives in Las Vegas, dear, and runs a resort."

"Oh!" Sean brightened visibly, "A dude ranch, huh?"

Rossi, having nodded to Joseph, sat down uncomfortably on the foot of the bed. "Not exactly, kid. But if you an' your Mom'll visit me, I promise yuh can ride horses an' chase cows from mornin' till night. Is it a deal?" He sought Mira's eyes and held them with his own.

"Gee! Say yes, Mom!"

"Well—"

"Please, Mom? I'm so sick of that blamed ol' school. You wouldn't send me back now anyway. 'Sides, we—you need a change."

"Yeah—a new deal all around," said Rossi quietly. "How about it?"

"Perhaps a change is in order," murmured Mira, smiling back at him. There was certainty in her smile, and a new contentment.

"Gee!" cried Sean, turning abruptly, "A real ranch. Joe, what do you think . . . Hey, Mom! He's gone—Joe's gone!"

Rossi turned. "Guess I'll have to mail him a check for his services."

Then he turned back to Mira.

THE AUTHOR

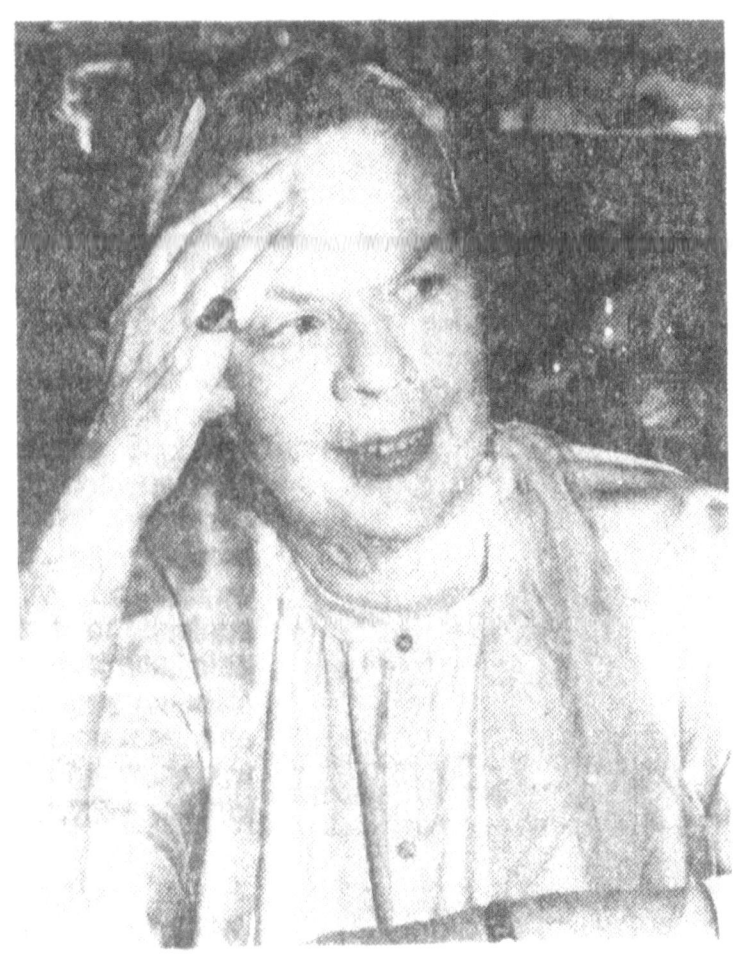

Elizabeth Taylor

COACHWHIP PUBLICATIONS
COACHWHIPBOOKS.COM

COACHWHIP PUBLICATIONS
CoachwhipBooks.com

THE JINX
THEATRE
MURDER

ALEXANDER WILLIAMS

COACHWHIP PUBLICATIONS
COACHWHIPBOOKS.COM

DEATH
OVER
NEWARK

ALEXANDER WILLIAMS

COACHWHIP PUBLICATIONS
CoachwhipBooks.com

MURDER
IN THE
WPA

ALEXANDER WILLIAMS

COACHWHIP PUBLICATIONS
CoachwhipBooks.com

COACHWHIP PUBLICATIONS
CoachwhipBooks.com

COACHWHIP PUBLICATIONS
CoachwhipBooks.com

MURDER
IN A WALLED TOWN
Katherine Woods

COACHWHIP PUBLICATIONS
CoachwhipBooks.com

www.ingramcontent.com/pod-product-compliance
Lightning Source LLC
Chambersburg PA
CBHW020643250626
47154CB00008B/2787